TEEN TITANS GO! TRAINING MANUAL

BY ERIC LUPER

PENGUIN YOUNG READERS LICENSES
An Imprint of Penguin Random House

DUDE, IF YOU ACTUALLY READ THIS PAGE, YOU ARE TOTALLY LAME.

BO-RING!!

PENGUIN YOUNG READERS LICENSES
An Imprint of Penguin Random House LLC

Copyright © 2017 DC Comics.
TEEN TITANS GO! and all related characters and elements
© & ™ DC Comics and Warner Bros. Entertainment Inc. (s17).
Published in 2017 by Penguin Young Readers Licenses, an imprint of
Penguin Random House LLC, 345 Hudson Street, New York, New York 10014.
Manufactured in China.

ISBN 9780399542268   10 9 8 7 6 5 4 3 2 1

DEAR APPLICANT,

THANK YOU FOR YOUR INTEREST IN JOINING THE TEEN TITANS. THERE ARE MANY JOB OPENINGS AT TITANS TOWER. THIS APPLICATION WILL HELP US DECIDE WHERE YOU WOULD BEST FIT IN, IF AT ALL. PLEASE TAKE THESE TESTS SERIOUSLY. YOUR FUTURE DEPENDS ON IT.

SINCERELY,

WHO SAYS ROBIN'S THE BOSS AROUND HERE?

ROBIN

HE DOES.

LEADER OF THE TEEN TITANS

3

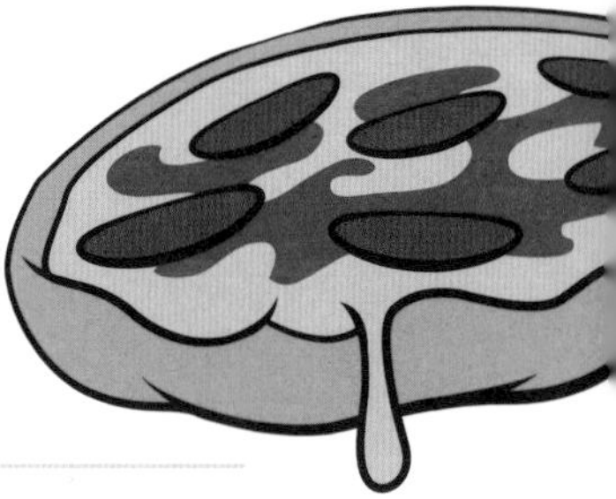

NAME: ____________

AGE: ____________

GENDER: ____________

SALARY REQUESTED: ____________

FAVORITE SPORT: ____________

FAVORITE TV SHOW: ____________

FAVORITE ANIMAL: ____________

FAVORITE FOOD: ____________

FAVORITE SONG: ____________

HAVE YOU EVER BEEN CONVICTED OF A CRIME? Yes No

IF YES, EXPLAIN: ____________

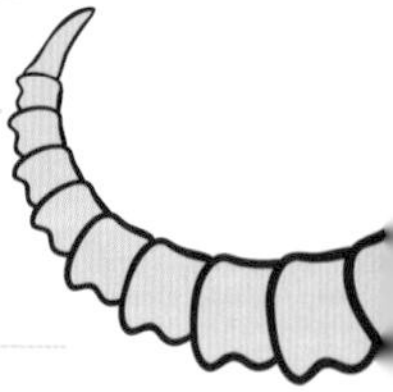

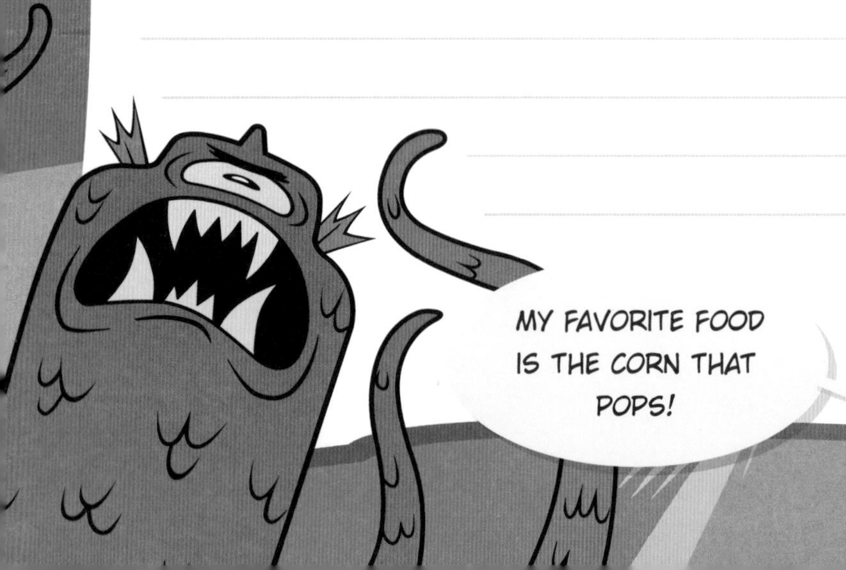
MY FAVORITE FOOD IS THE CORN THAT POPS!

NAME OF SCHOOL: ____________________

NAME OF PRESCHOOL: ____________________

NAME OF DAYCARE: ____________________

IF YOU HAD A PET MONKEY, WHAT WOULD YOU NAME IT?

____

IF YOU COULD HAVE ANY SUPERPOWER, WHAT WOULD IT BE AND WHY?

____

____

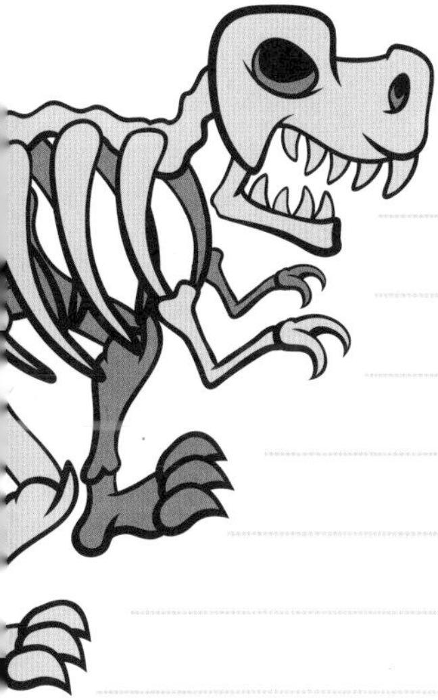

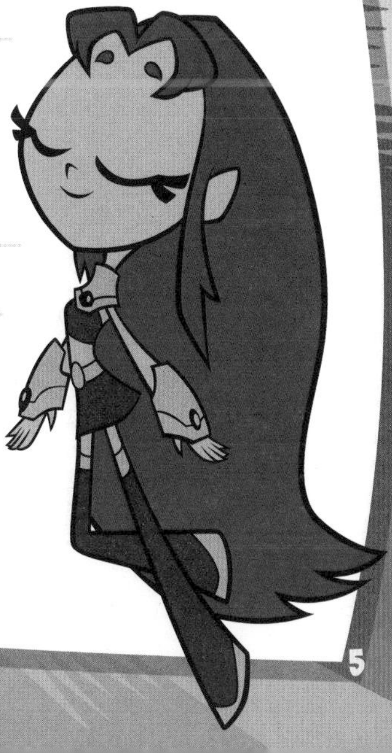

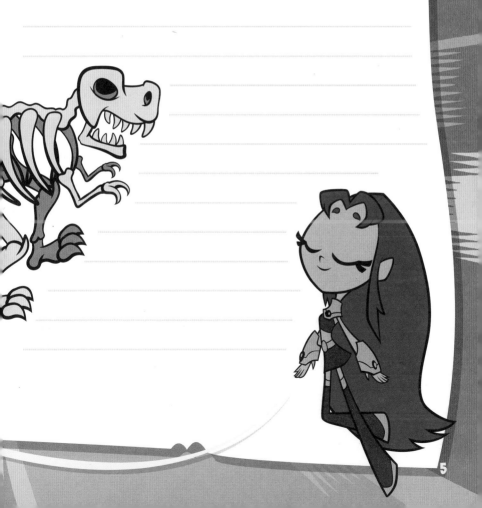

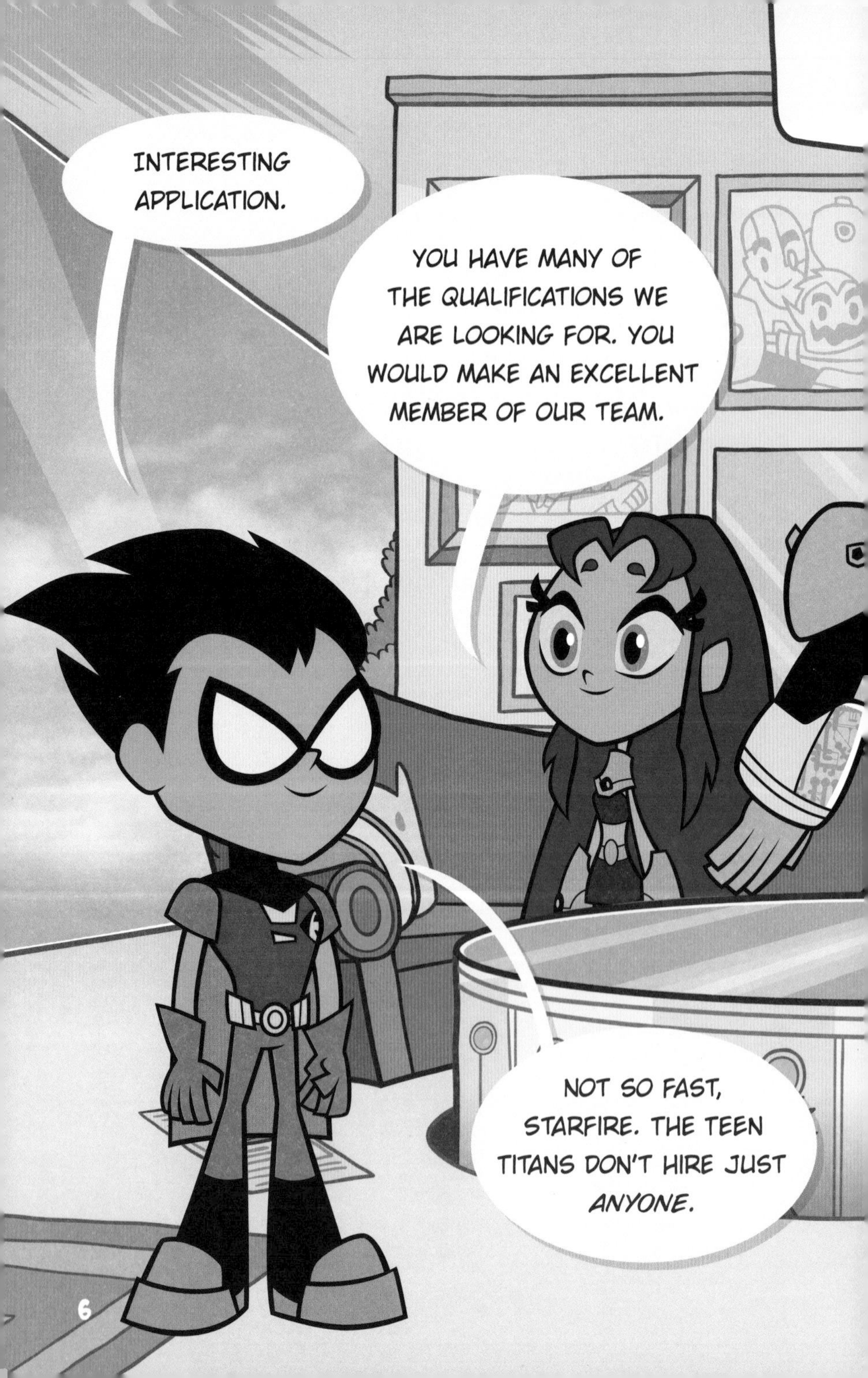
INTERESTING APPLICATION.
YOU HAVE MANY OF THE QUALIFICATIONS WE ARE LOOKING FOR. YOU WOULD MAKE AN EXCELLENT MEMBER OF OUR TEAM.
NOT SO FAST, STARFIRE. THE TEEN TITANS DON'T HIRE JUST *ANYONE*.

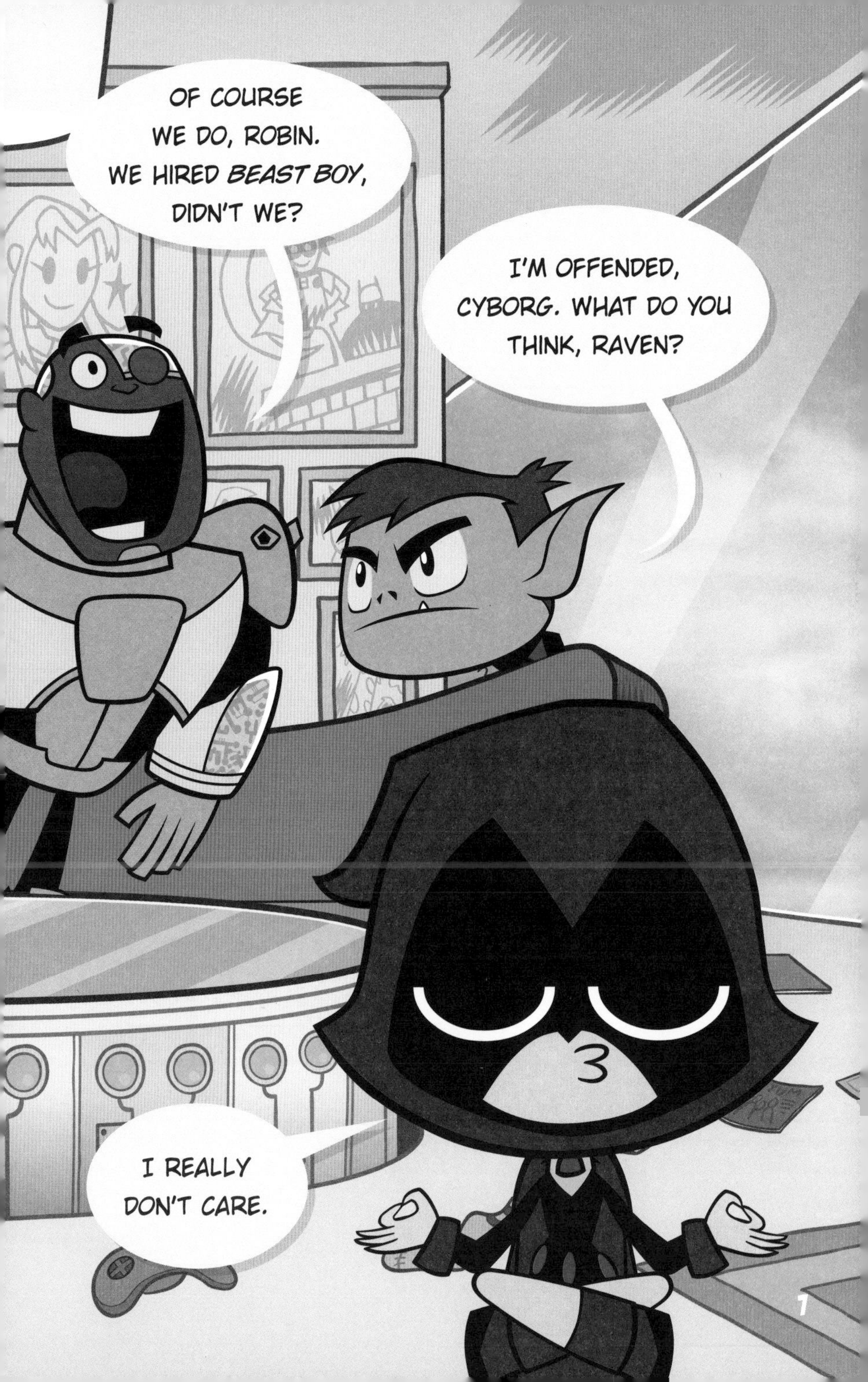
OF COURSE WE DO, ROBIN. WE HIRED *BEAST BOY*, DIDN'T WE?
I'M OFFENDED, CYBORG. WHAT DO YOU THINK, RAVEN?
I REALLY DON'T CARE.

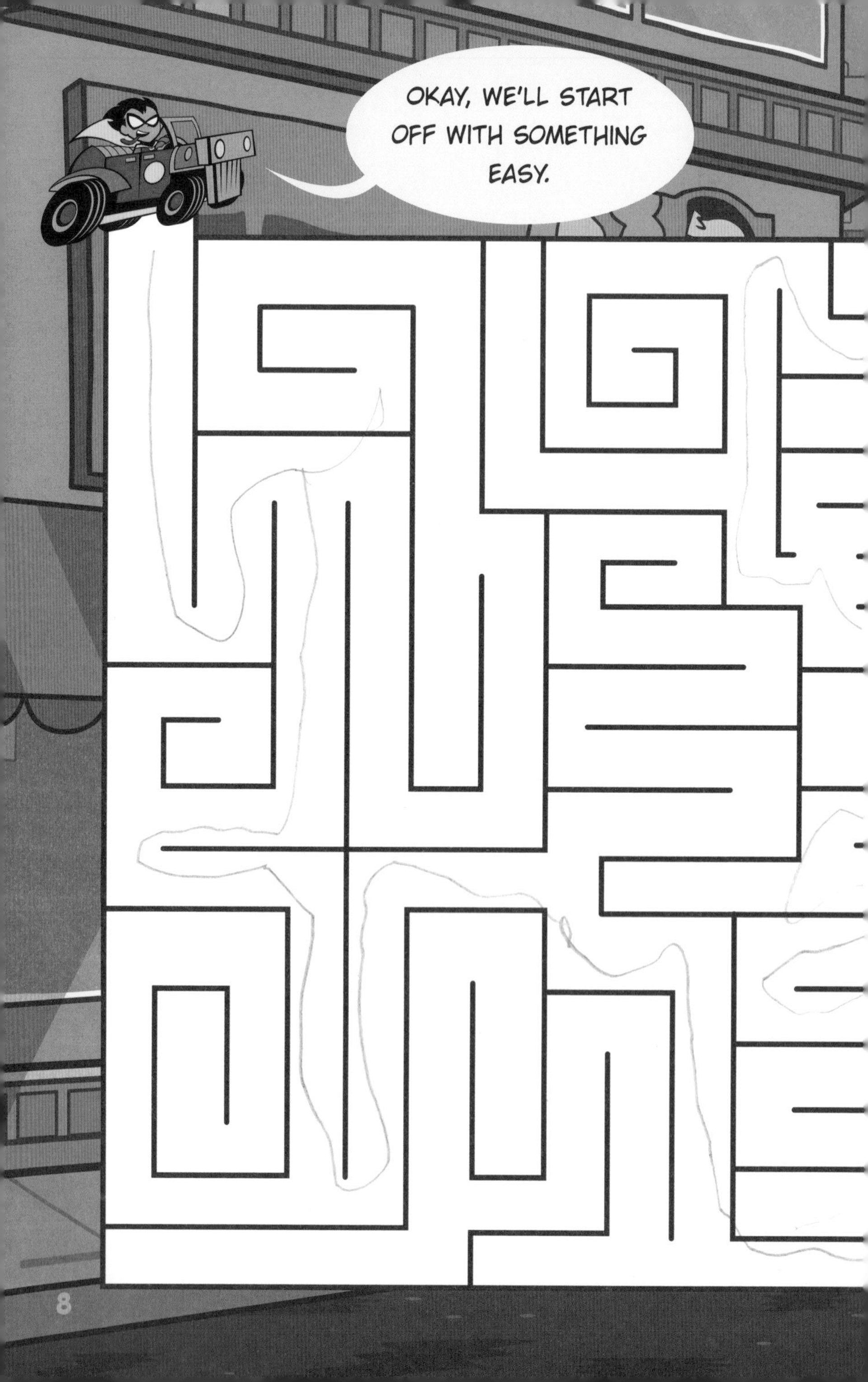
OKAY, WE'LL START OFF WITH SOMETHING EASY.

HELP GET THE T-CAR THROUGH WINDING CITY STREETS BACK TO TITANS TOWER. THE FASTER THE BETTER!

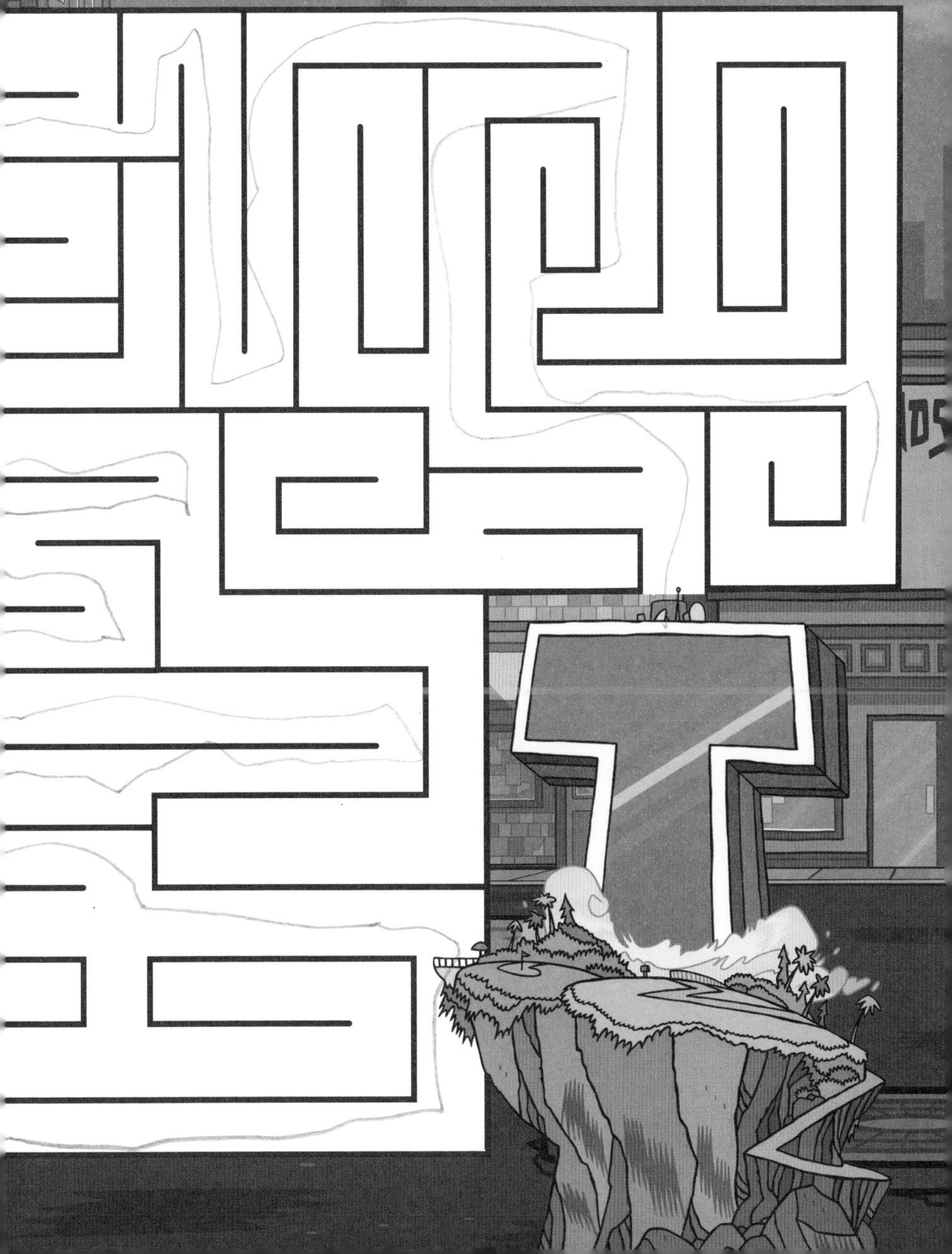

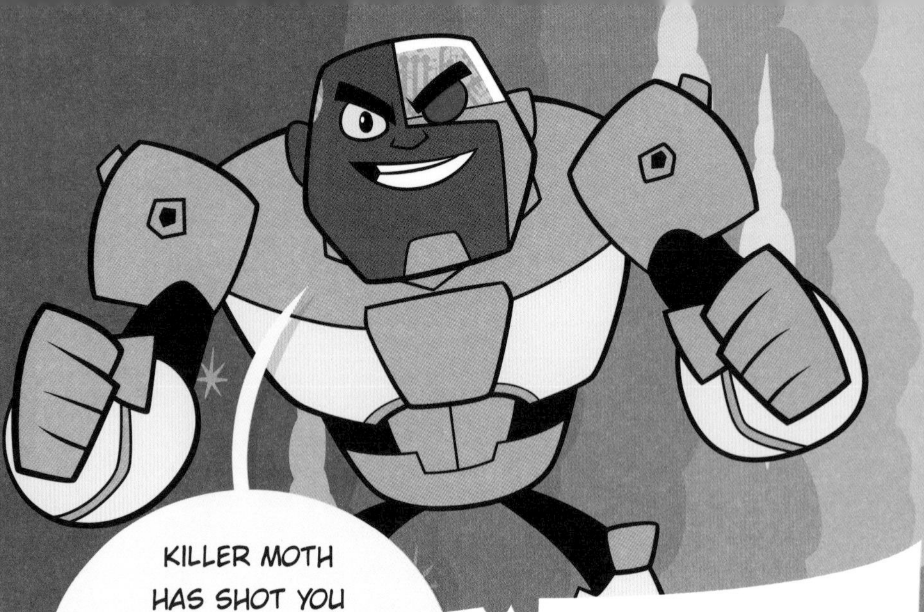
KILLER MOTH HAS SHOT YOU WITH THE BUG BEAM, MUTATING YOU INTO AN UGLY BUG CREATURE. DESCRIBE WHAT YOU LOOK LIKE!

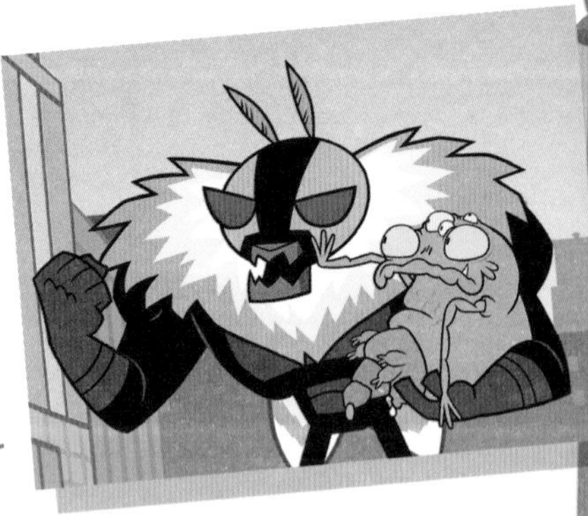

ANTENNAE: yes no

EYES: normal buggy other

WINGS: yes no

ARMS: normal pincers claws other

BODY: normal creepy ant body centipede segments other

LEGS: none normal spiked suction cups other

DEFENSE: webs acid barf club tail other

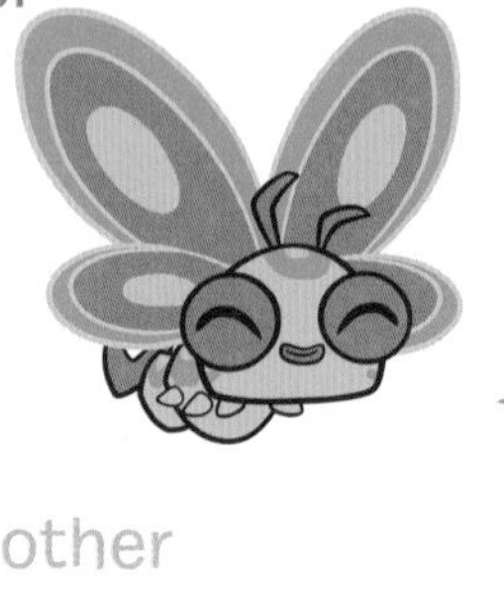

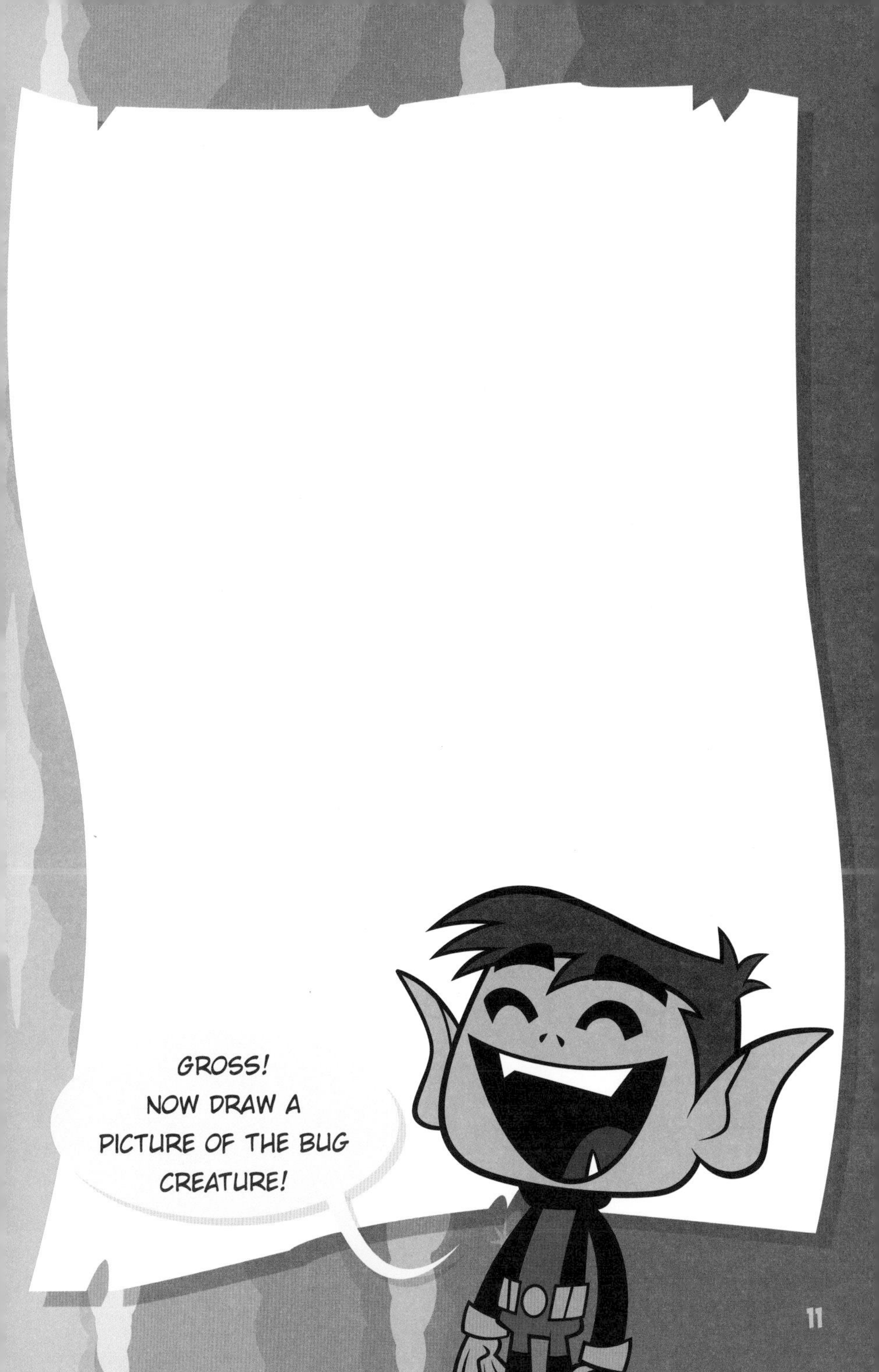
GROSS!
NOW DRAW A
PICTURE OF THE BUG
CREATURE!

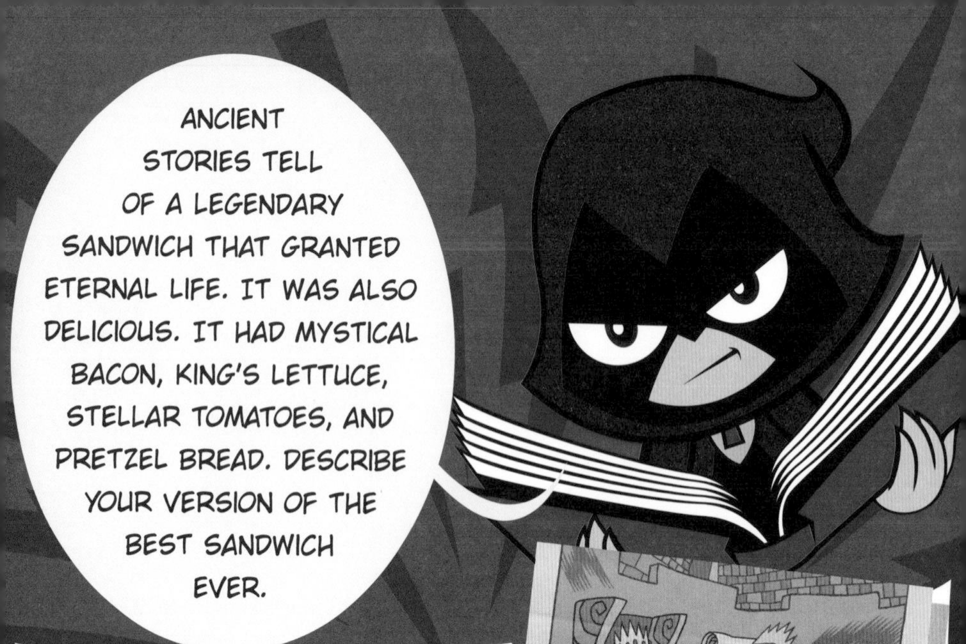
ANCIENT STORIES TELL OF A LEGENDARY SANDWICH THAT GRANTED ETERNAL LIFE. IT WAS ALSO DELICIOUS. IT HAD MYSTICAL BACON, KING'S LETTUCE, STELLAR TOMATOES, AND PRETZEL BREAD. DESCRIBE YOUR VERSION OF THE BEST SANDWICH EVER.

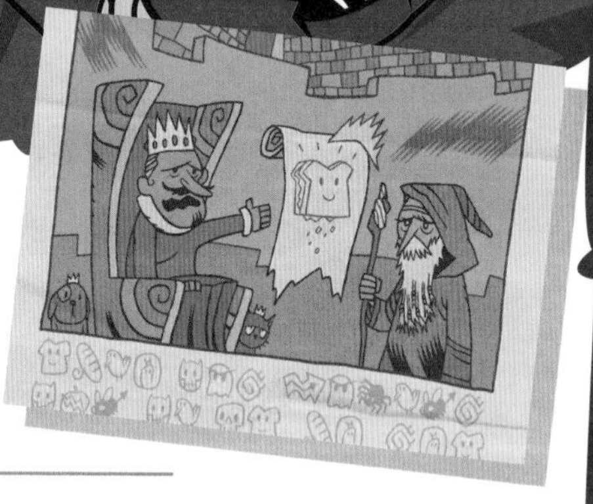

BREAD: ______________________

____

FILLINGS: ______________________

____

____

TOPPINGS: ______________________

____

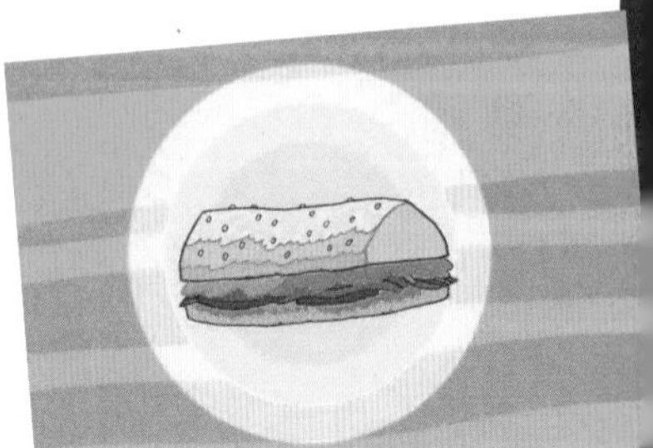

SIDE DISHES: ______________________

____

DRINK: ______________________

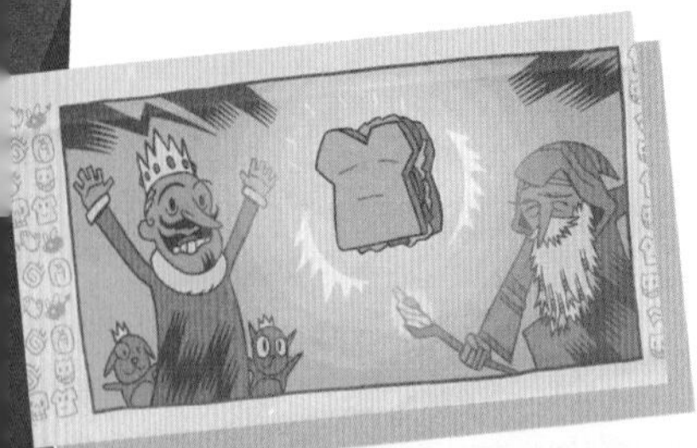

____

____

____

ROBIN TELLS JOKES SO BAD ONLY AN UNCLE WOULD TELL THEM:

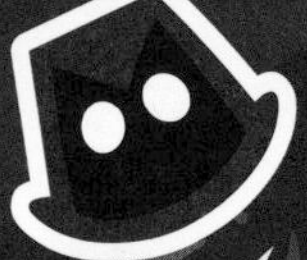

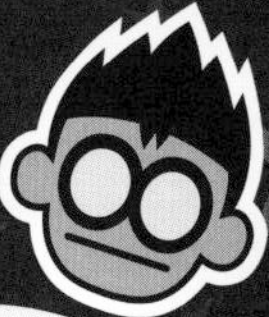

HOW DO YOU WANT YOUR STEAK COOKED?

ON A STOVE! BOOM!

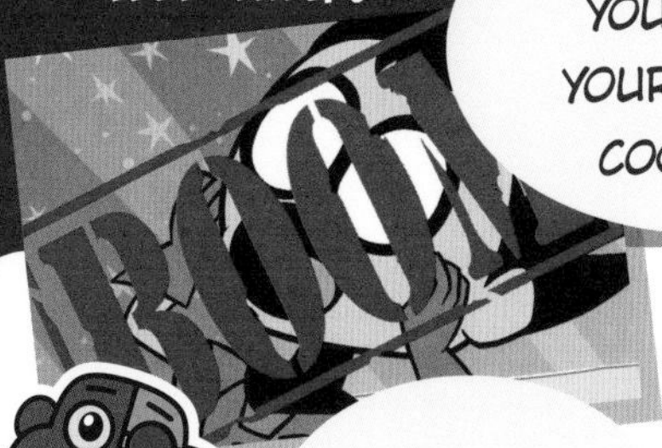

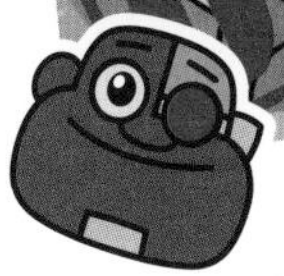

MAN, I'M HUNGRY.

NICE TO MEET YOU, HUNGRY. I'M ROBIN. BOOM!

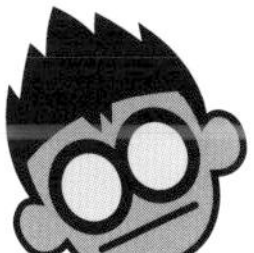

THINK OF YOUR OWN UNCLE JOKES AND WRITE THEM DOWN.

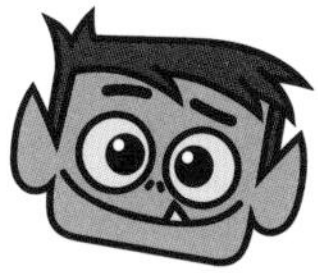

IF YOU CAN'T THINK OF ONE, GO ASK YOUR UNCLE!

ONCE, RAVEN MADE AN EXACT COPY OF CYBORG IN ORDER TO PLAY THE GAME OF CAVEMEN AND DINOSAURS WITH BEAST BOY. IF YOU HAD AN EXACT COPY OF YOURSELF, WHAT WOULD YOU HAVE HIM OR HER DO FOR YOU? WRITE A SHORT STORY ABOUT THAT!

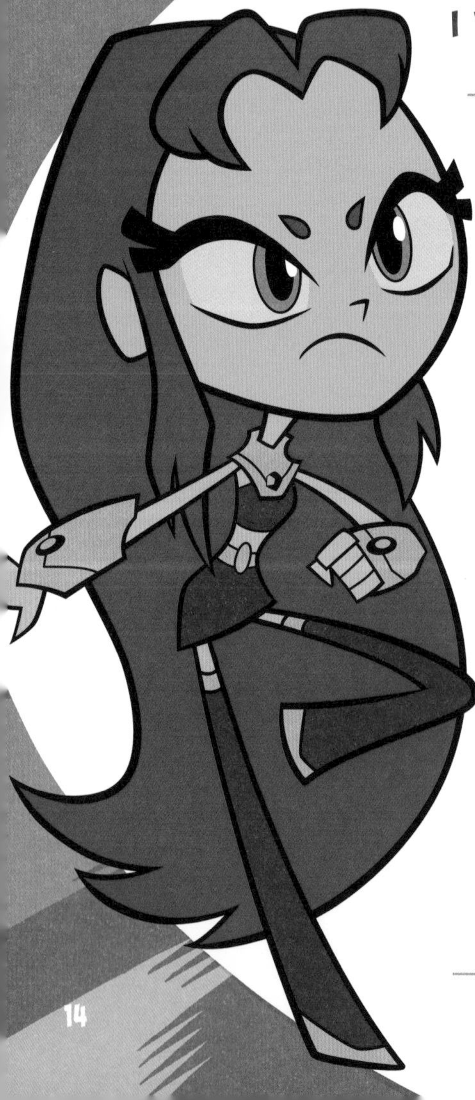

I TOTALLY DIDN'T FEEL LIKE . . .

WORD SEARCH!

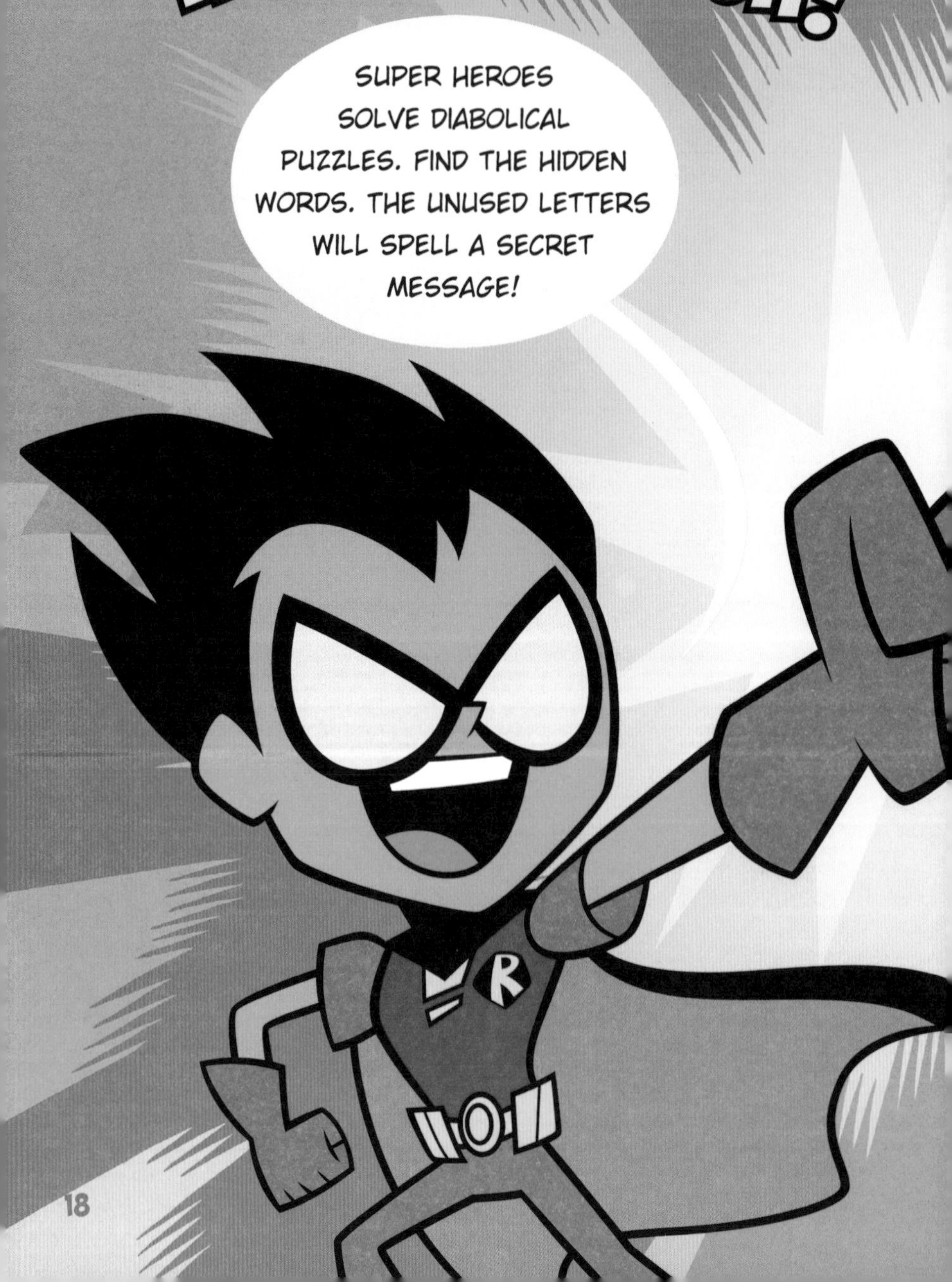
SUPER HEROES SOLVE DIABOLICAL PUZZLES. FIND THE HIDDEN WORDS. THE UNUSED LETTERS WILL SPELL A SECRET MESSAGE!

Word Search

```
C A Q U A L A D S T
Y N A Z T H I V E E E
B E A S T B O Y Y E N
O V A R U I T M D M T
R A R P I M M Z E O I
G R R E M A I G E R T
A N T R E N S G P R A
M A M M O T H S S N
X N I J S R O B I N
G O E R I F R A T S
```

AQUALAD

BEAST BOY

CYBORG

GIZMO

HIVE

JINX

MAMMOTH

MAS

MENOS

RAVEN

ROBIN

SEE-MORE

SPEEDY

STARFIRE

SUPER

TEEN TITANS

TERRA

ZAN

SECRET MESSAGE: _ _ _ _ _ _ _ _ _   (TITANS GO)

19

When the Teen Titans get bored, Raven tells them to try reading a book.

What is the best book you've ever read?

What made it so great?

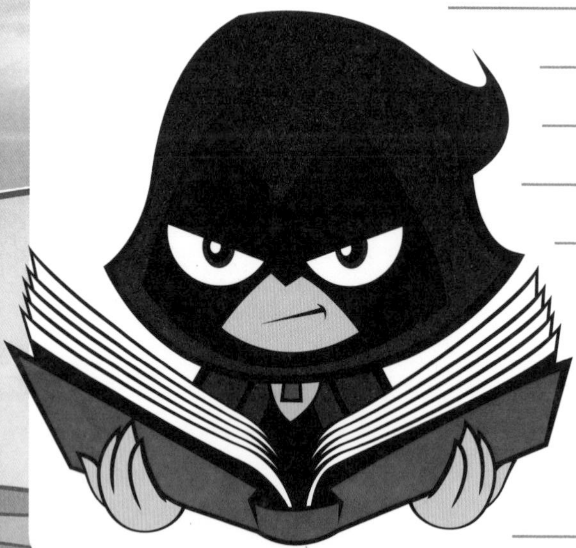

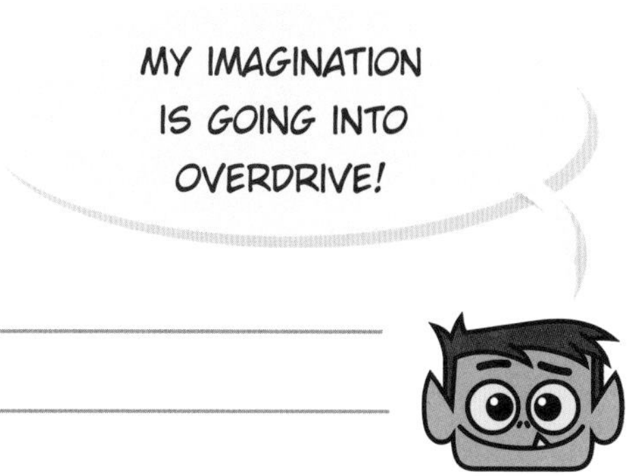
MY IMAGINATION IS GOING INTO OVERDRIVE!

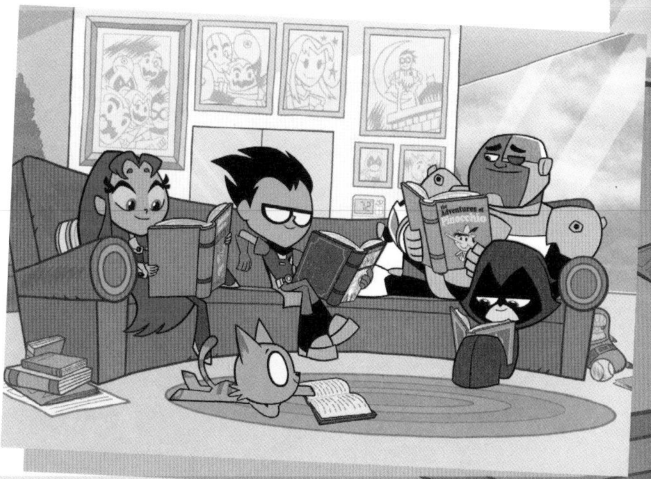

Beast Boy can transform into any animal. If you could transform into any animal, what would it be and why?

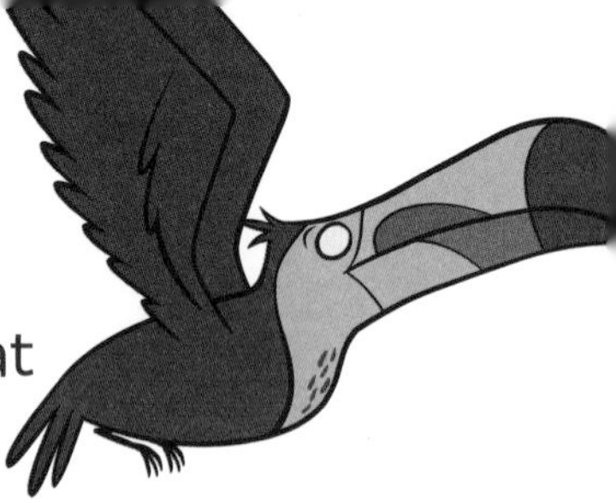

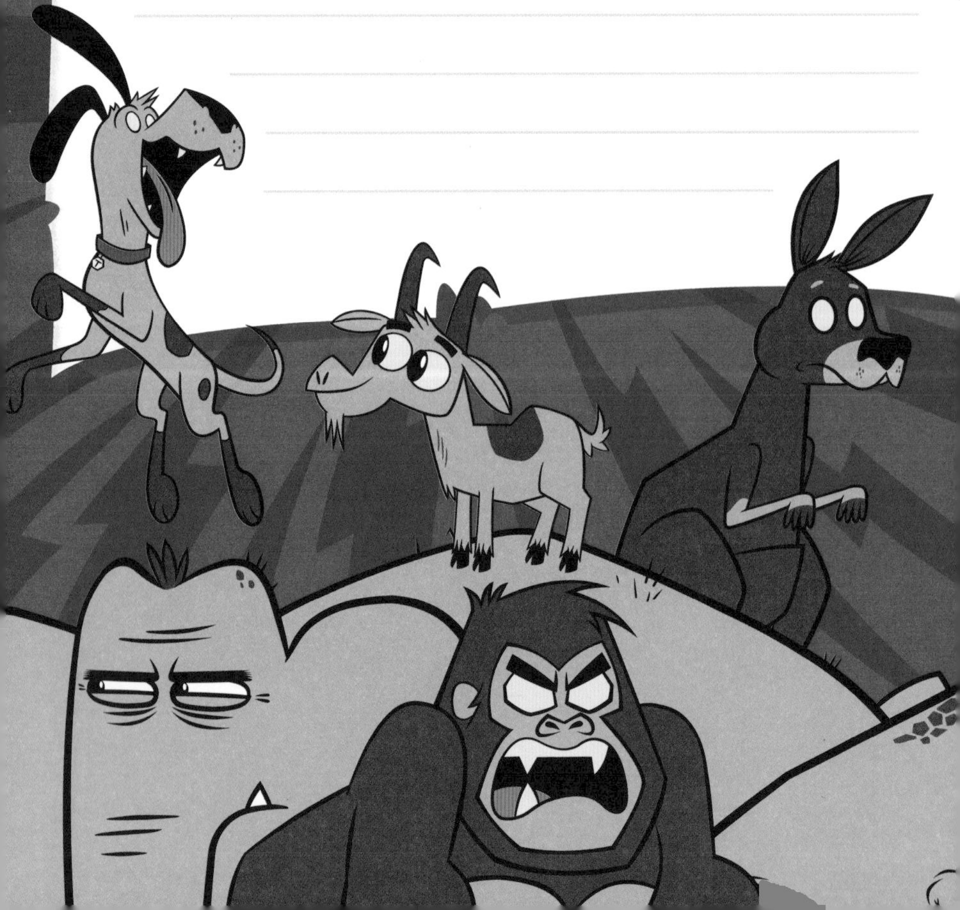

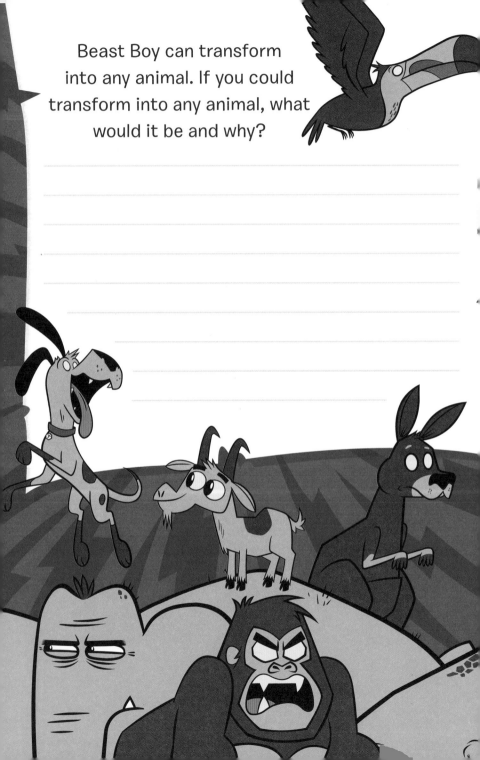

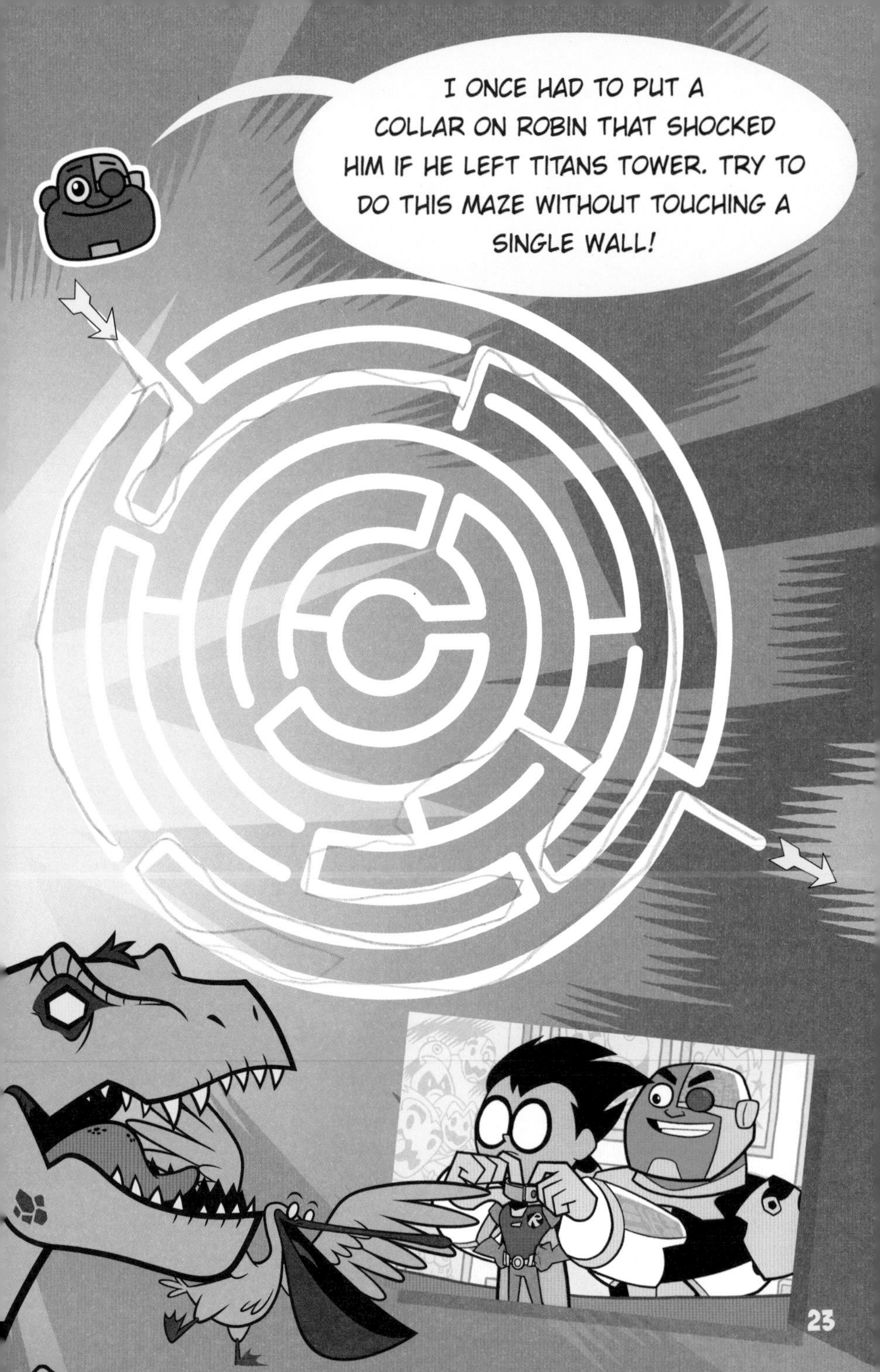
I ONCE HAD TO PUT A COLLAR ON ROBIN THAT SHOCKED HIM IF HE LEFT TITANS TOWER. TRY TO DO THIS MAZE WITHOUT TOUCHING A SINGLE WALL!

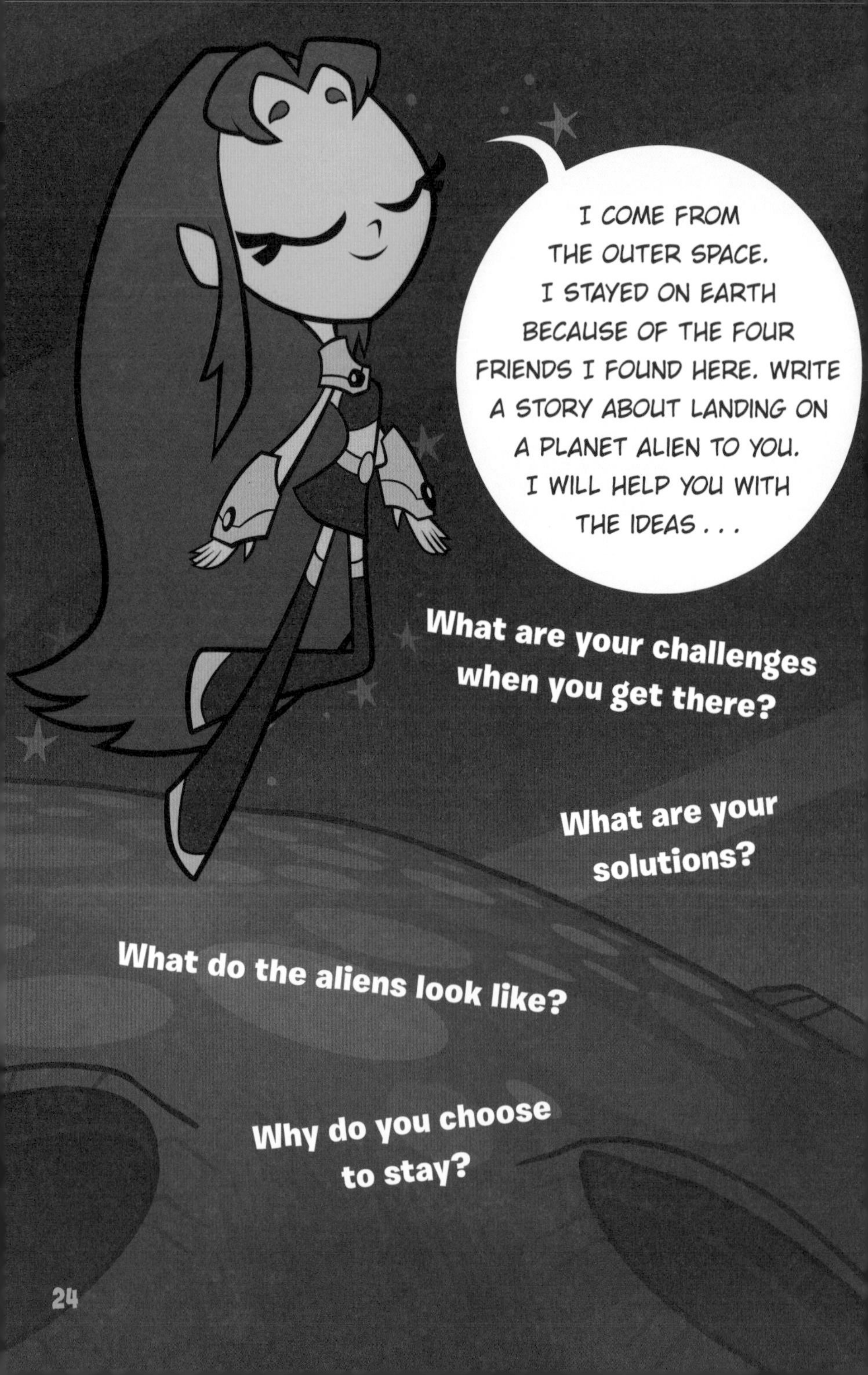
I COME FROM THE OUTER SPACE. I STAYED ON EARTH BECAUSE OF THE FOUR FRIENDS I FOUND HERE. WRITE A STORY ABOUT LANDING ON A PLANET ALIEN TO YOU. I WILL HELP YOU WITH THE IDEAS . . .

What are your challenges when you get there?

What are your solutions?

What do the aliens look like?

Why do you choose to stay?

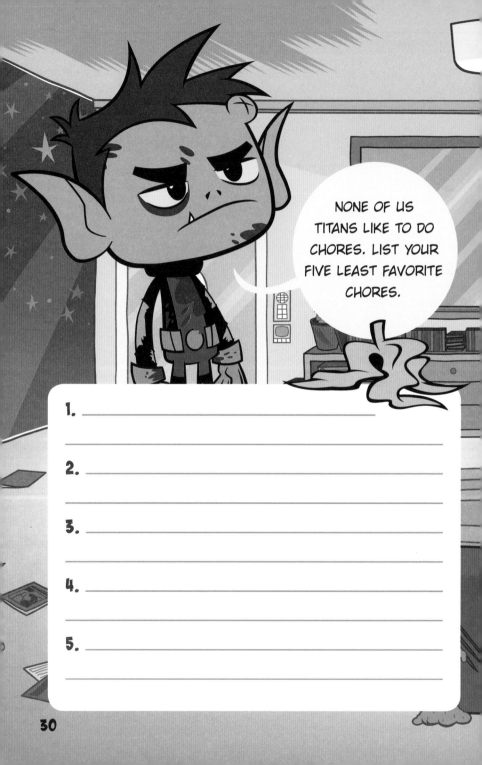

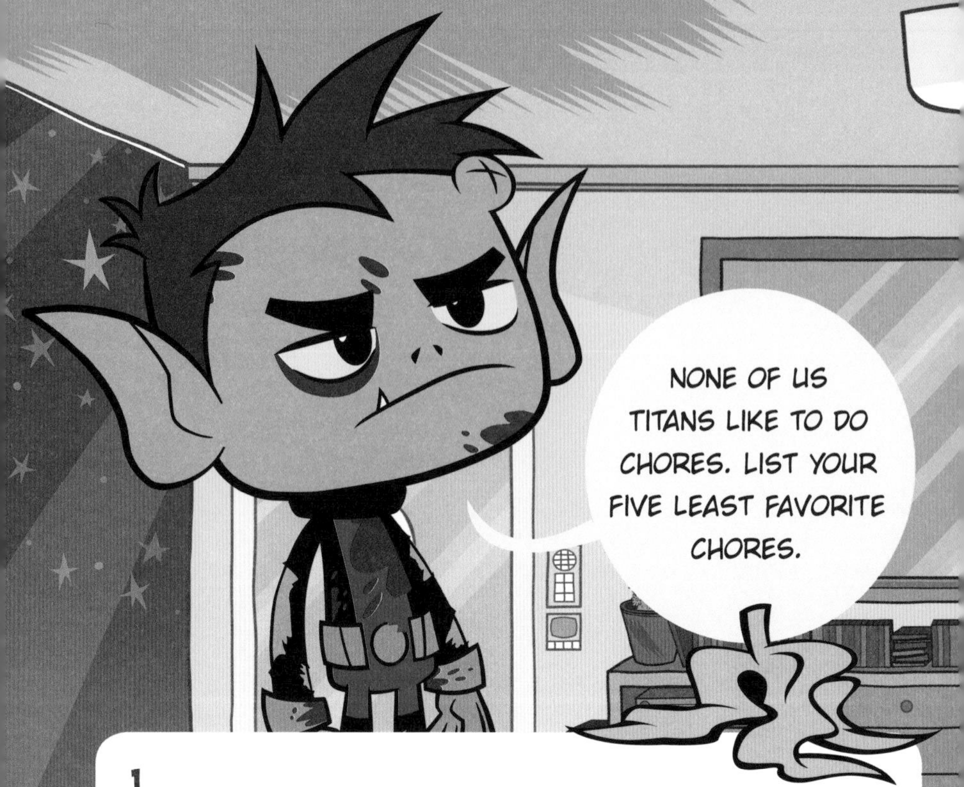
NONE OF US TITANS LIKE TO DO CHORES. LIST YOUR FIVE LEAST FAVORITE CHORES.

1. ______________________________

____

2. ______________________________

____

3. ______________________________

____

4. ______________________________

____

5. ______________________________

____

NOW DRAW A
ROBOT SPECIFICALLY
DESIGNED TO DO THOSE
CHORES!

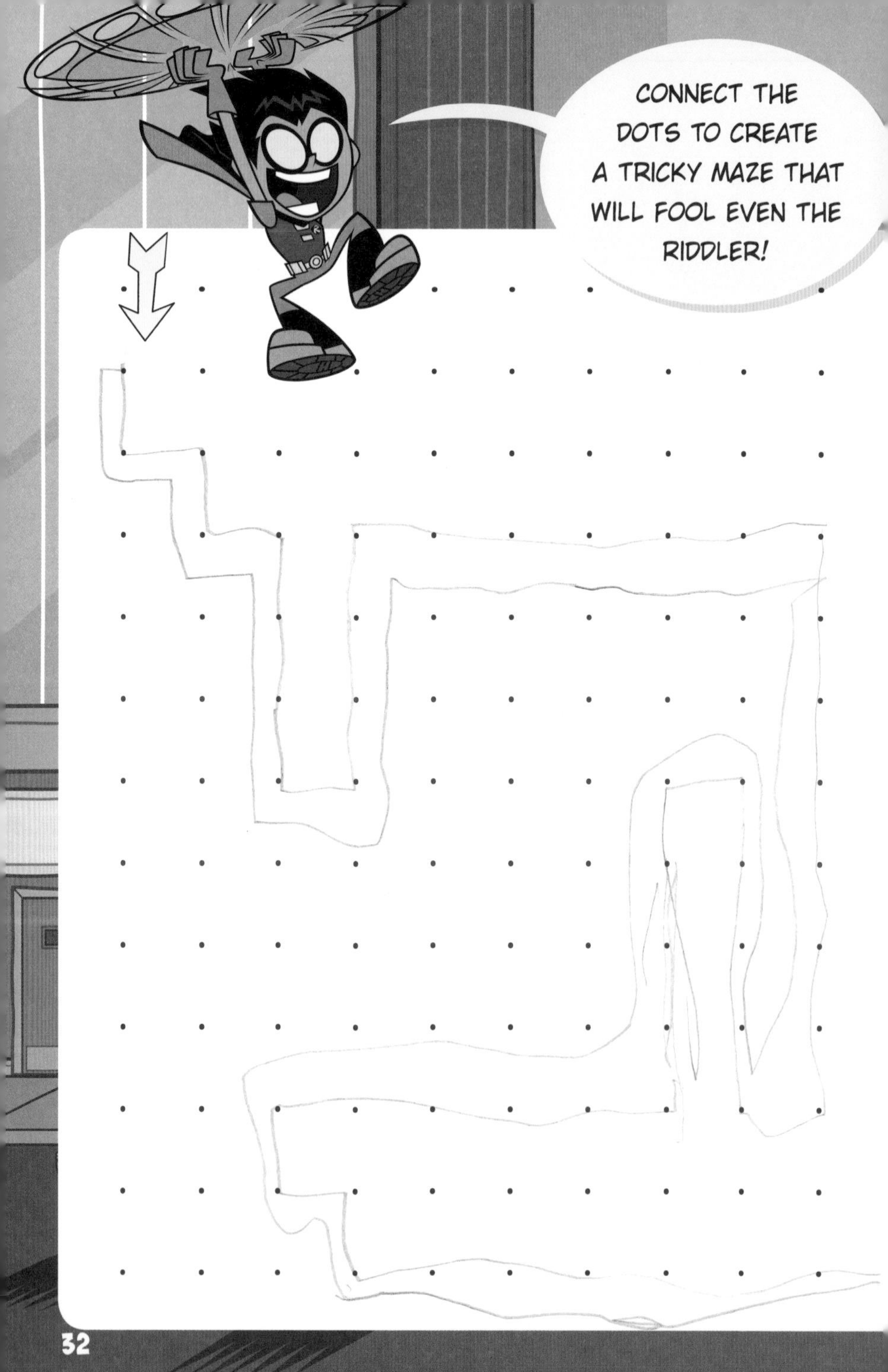
CONNECT THE DOTS TO CREATE A TRICKY MAZE THAT WILL FOOL EVEN THE RIDDLER!

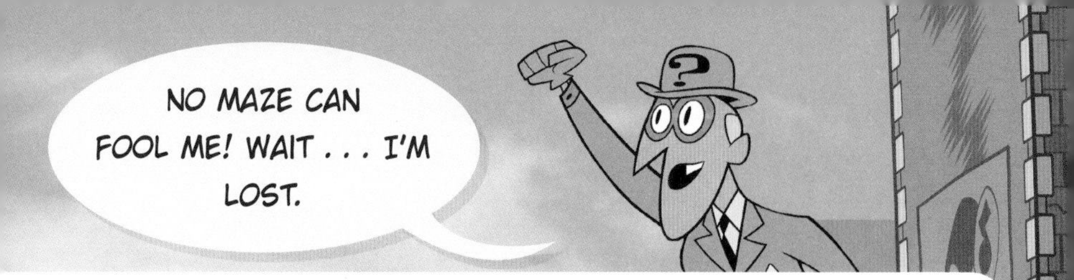
NO MAZE CAN FOOL ME! WAIT . . . I'M LOST.

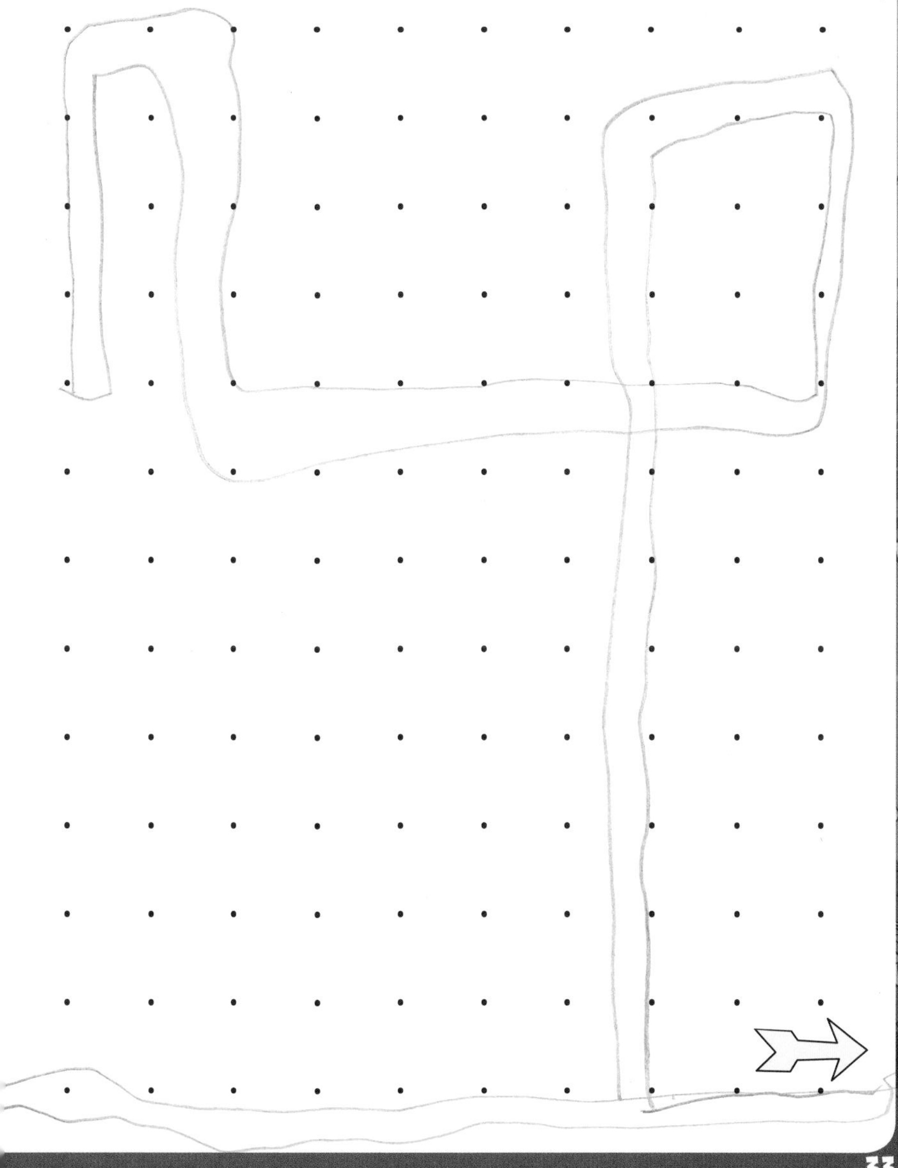

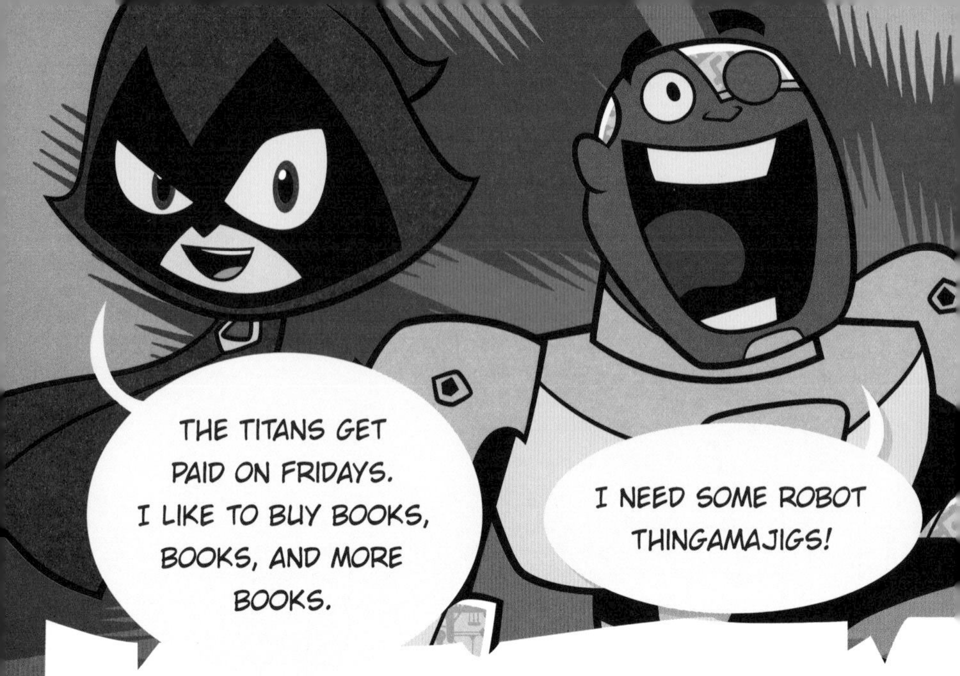
THE TITANS GET PAID ON FRIDAYS. I LIKE TO BUY BOOKS, BOOKS, AND MORE BOOKS.
I NEED SOME ROBOT THINGAMAJIGS!

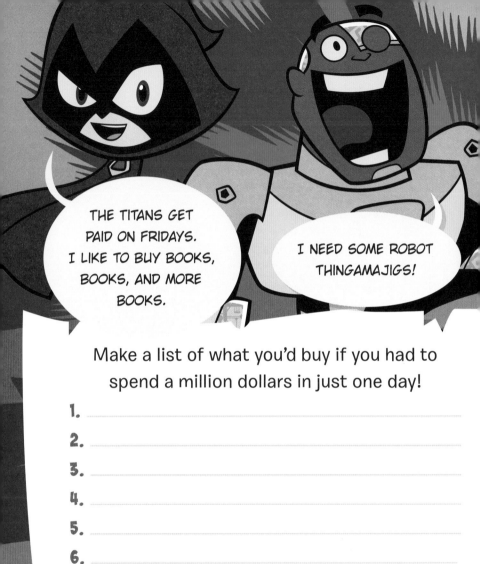

Make a list of what you'd buy if you had to spend a million dollars in just one day!

1. ______
2. ______
3. ______
4. ______
5. ______
6. ______
7. ______
8. ______
9. ______
10. ______

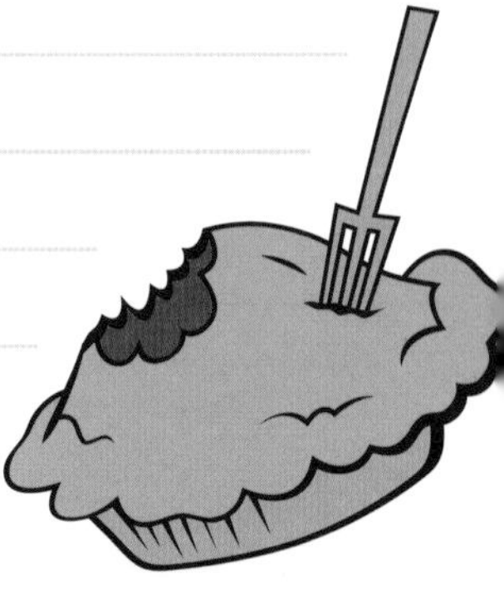

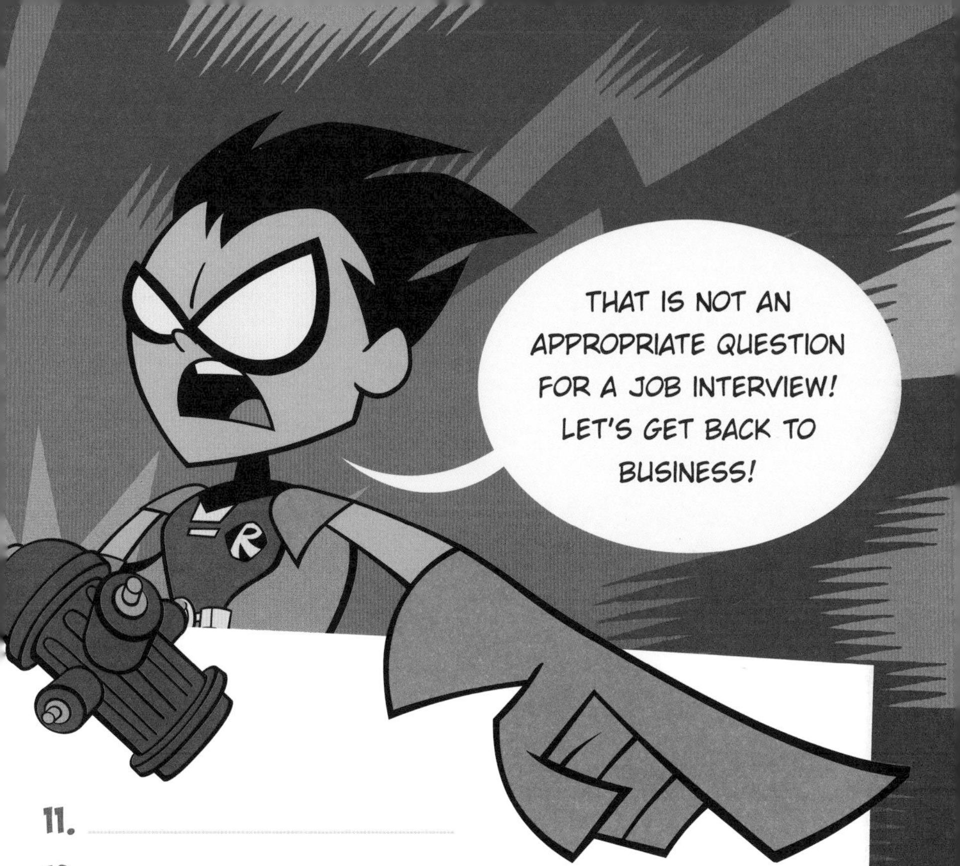
THAT IS NOT AN APPROPRIATE QUESTION FOR A JOB INTERVIEW! LET'S GET BACK TO BUSINESS!

11. ______________________

12. ______________________

13. ______________________

14. ______________________

15. ______________________

16. ______________________

17. ______________________

18. ______________________

19. ______________________

20. ______________________

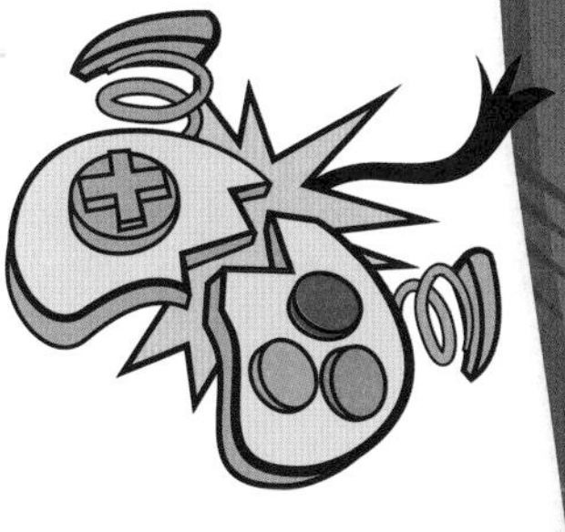

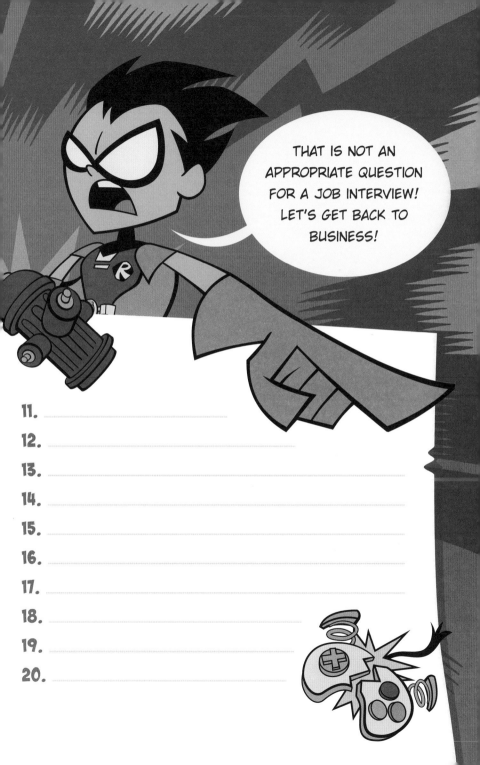

Unscramble these words to discover the Teen Titans' most dangerous foes!

MOGZI ______	DIDRLER ______
DALES ______	SLAPSUM ______
RAFICLEKB ______	REEMOSE reemose
ROJEK ______	XINJ Jinx

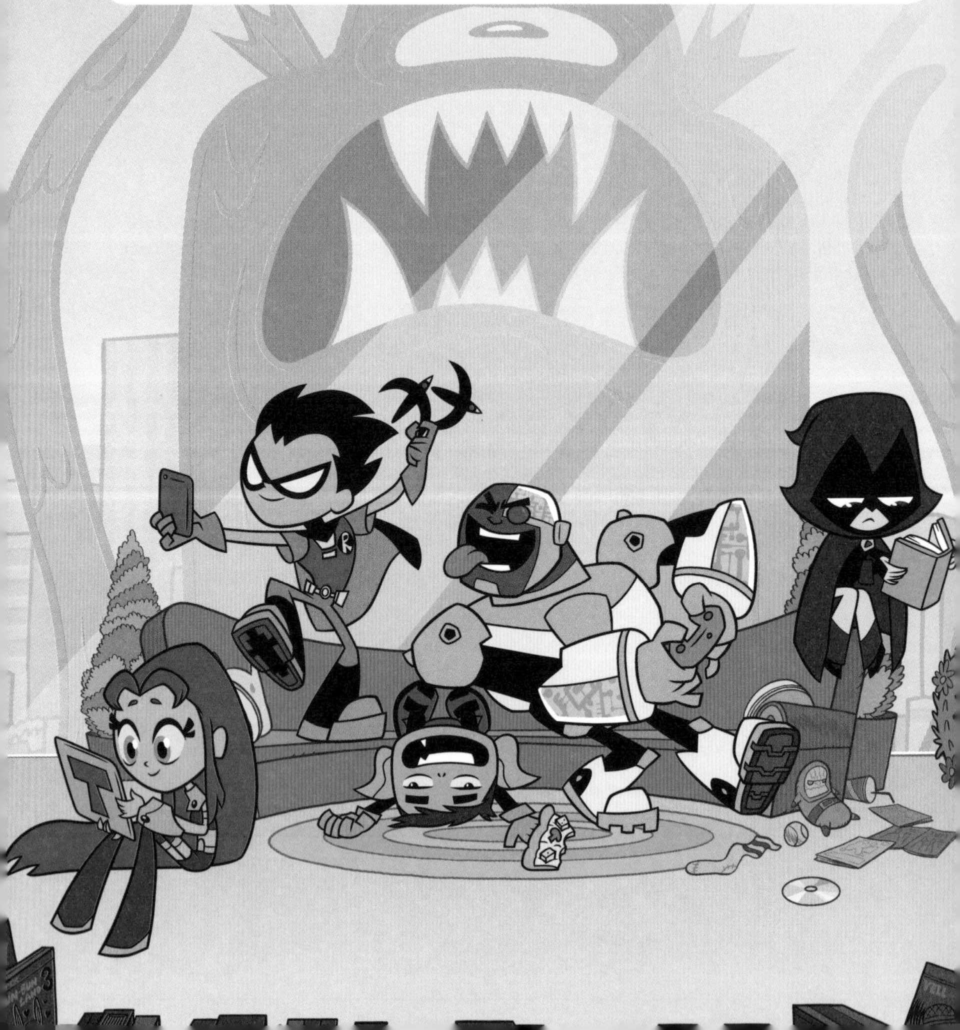

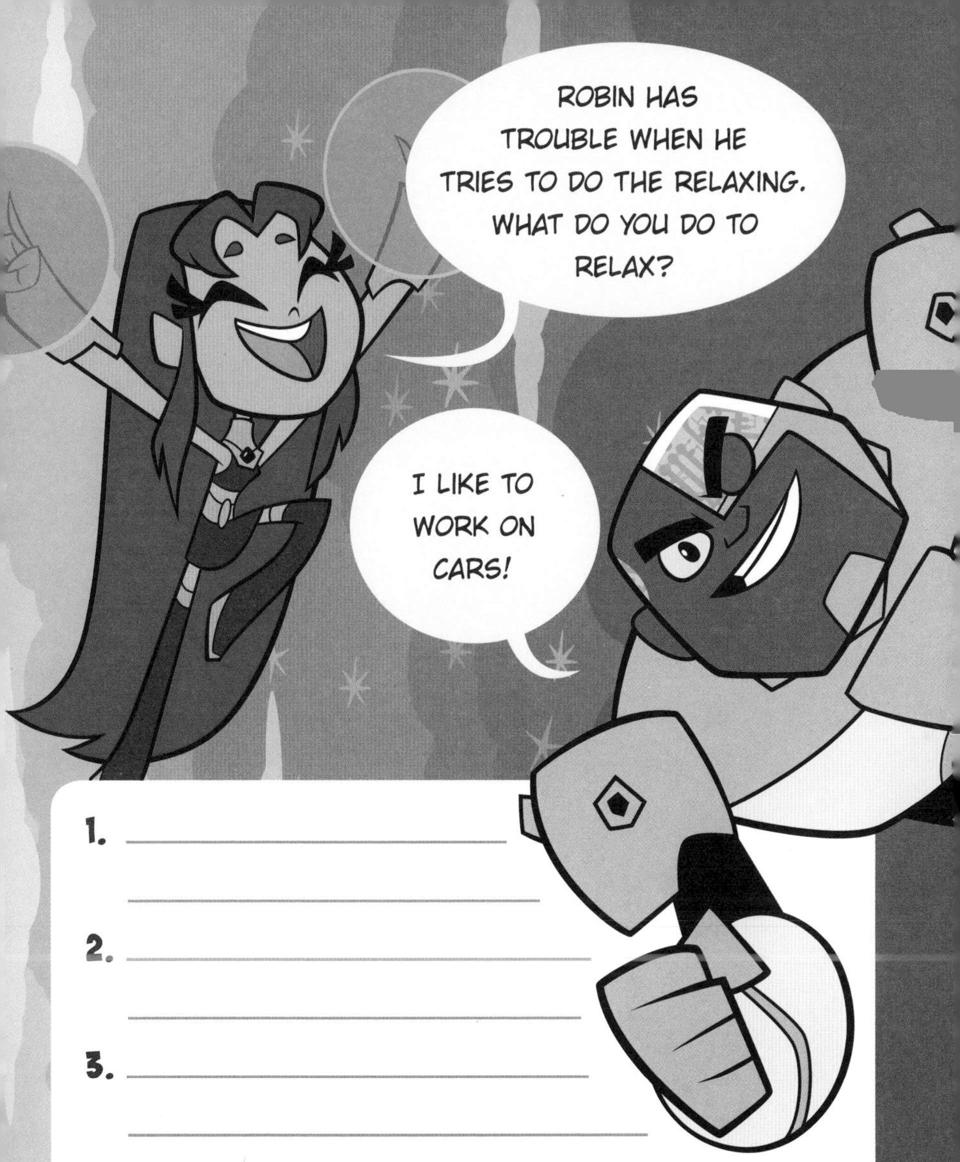
ROBIN HAS TROUBLE WHEN HE TRIES TO DO THE RELAXING. WHAT DO YOU DO TO RELAX?
I LIKE TO WORK ON CARS!

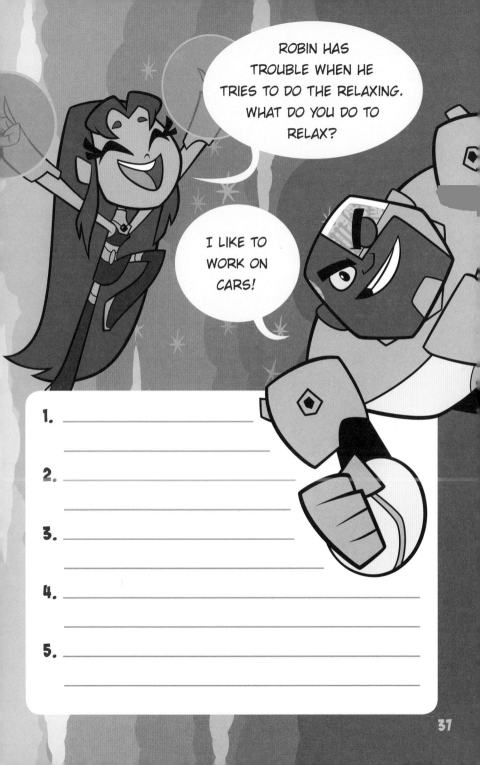

1. ______________________________

2. ______________________________

3. ______________________________

4. ______________________________

5. ______________________________

Once, Lady Legasus took over the Teen Titans. She made everyone do exercises to strengthen their legs. What would your "LEGGY" super hero name be? What would be your special move? Take this test to find out!

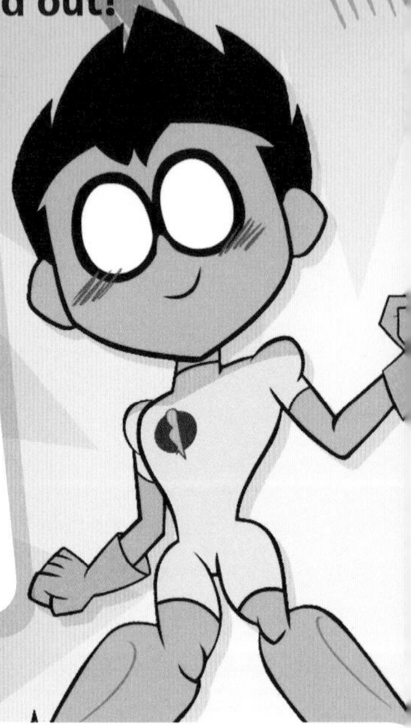

First Name

First Letter of First Name

A to D: Captain

E to I: The Incredible

J to M: Generalissimo

N to Q: Stinky

R to U: Speedy

V to Z: The Massive

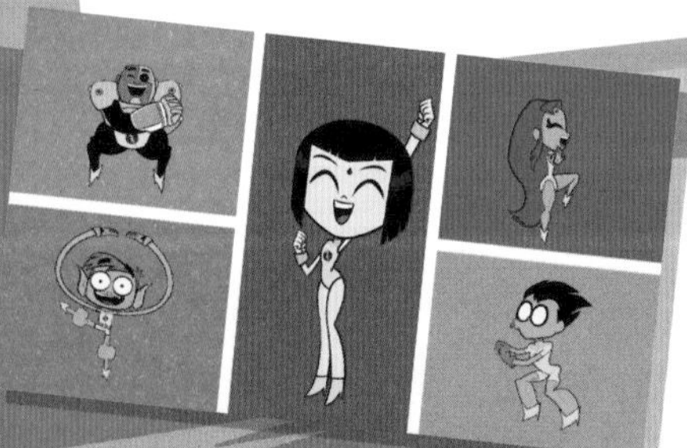

Middle Name

Last Letter of First Name

A to D: Quad-Buster

E to I: Hammy-Slammy

J to M: Knee-Crusher

N to Q: Twinkletoes

R to U: Ankle-Twister

V to Z: Calf-Smasher

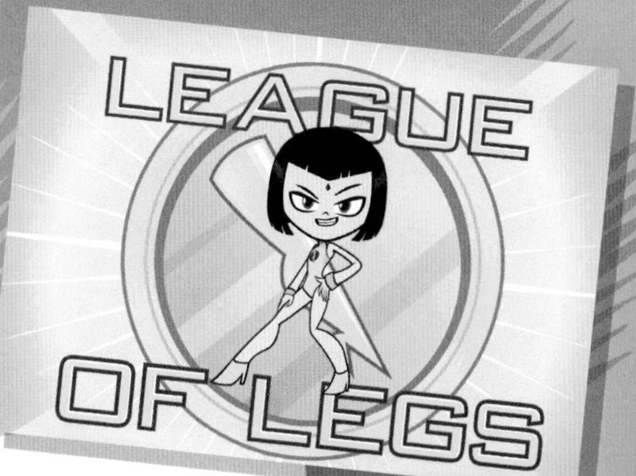
LEAGUE
OF LEGS

Special Move
First Letter of Last Name
A to D: Killer Dropkick
E to I: Rockin' Roundhouse
J to M: Scissor Slice
N to Q: Hip Flip
R to U: Buttock Bump
V to Z: Spinning Superpower Split

Last Name
Last Letter of Last Name
A to D: The Destroyer
E to I: The Unstoppable
J to M: The Sprinter
N to Q: Quick Slick
R to U: Power Squat
V to Z: Lungemeister

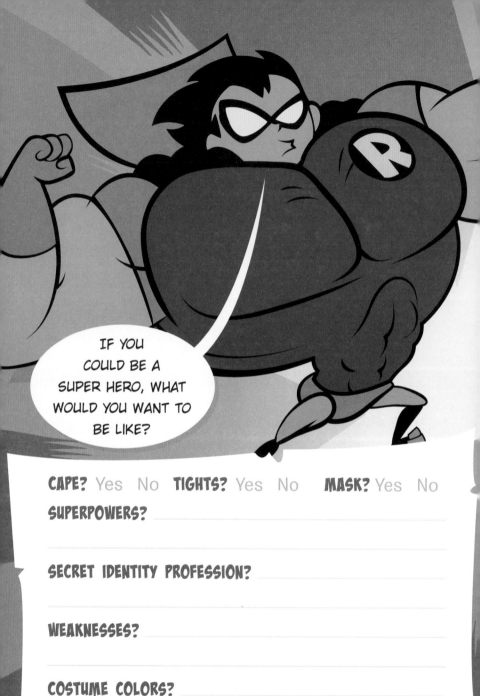

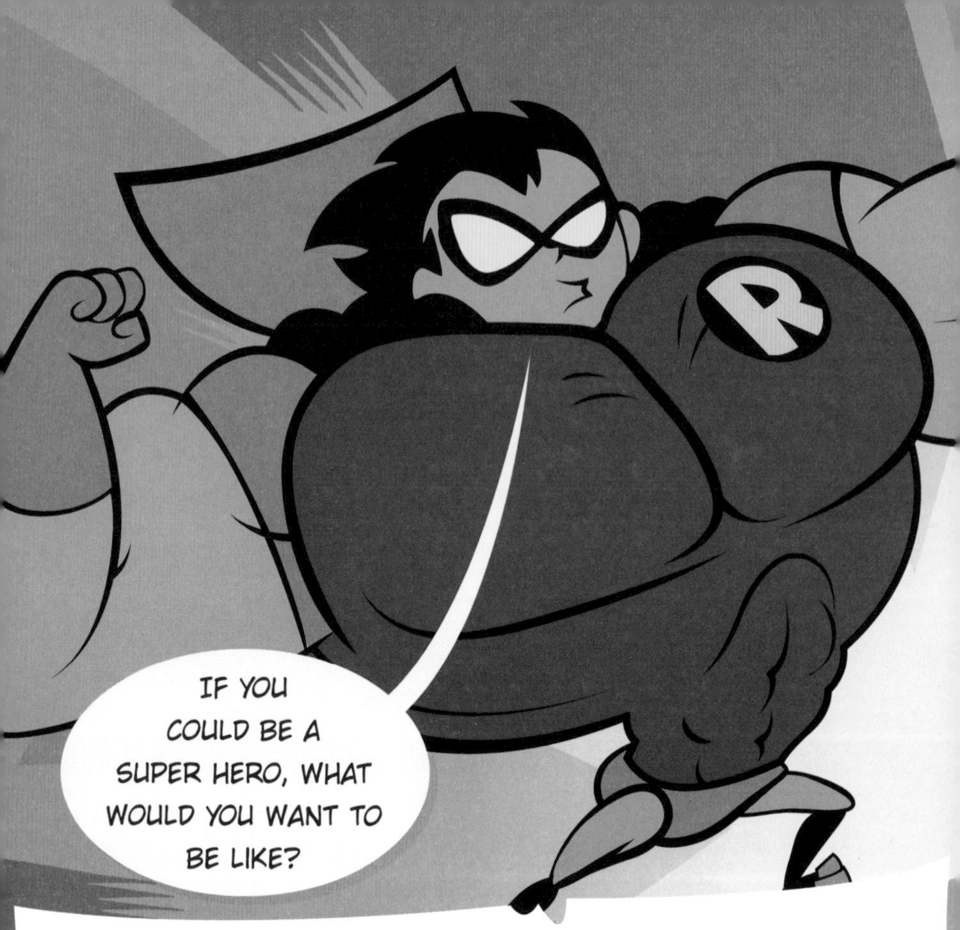
IF YOU COULD BE A SUPER HERO, WHAT WOULD YOU WANT TO BE LIKE?

CAPE? Yes No **TIGHTS?** Yes No **MASK?** Yes No

SUPERPOWERS? ______________________________

____

SECRET IDENTITY PROFESSION? ______________________________

____

WEAKNESSES? ______________________________

____

COSTUME COLORS? ______________________________

____

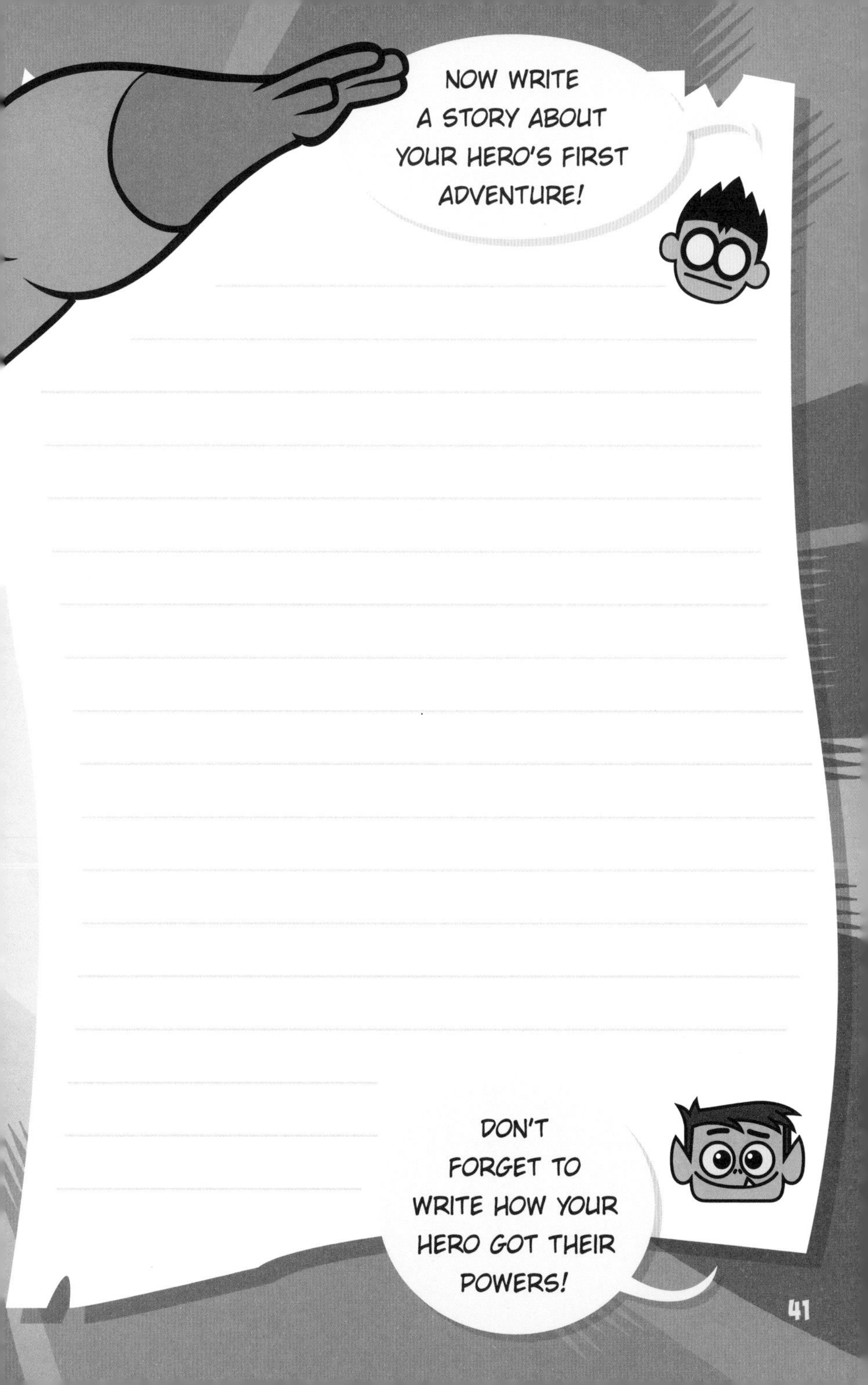
NOW WRITE A STORY ABOUT YOUR HERO'S FIRST ADVENTURE!
DON'T FORGET TO WRITE HOW YOUR HERO GOT THEIR POWERS!

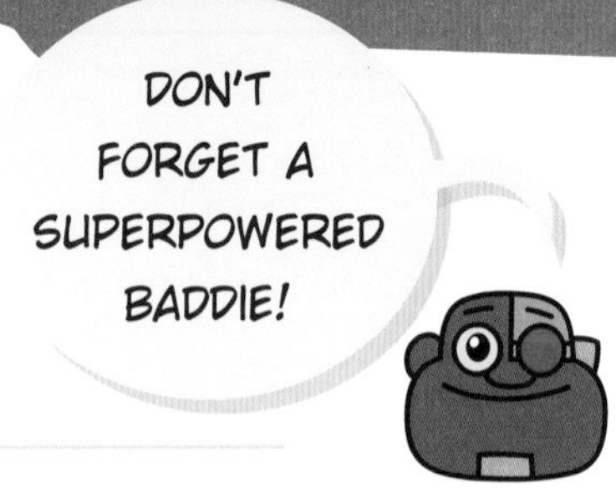
DON'T FORGET A SUPERPOWERED BADDIE!

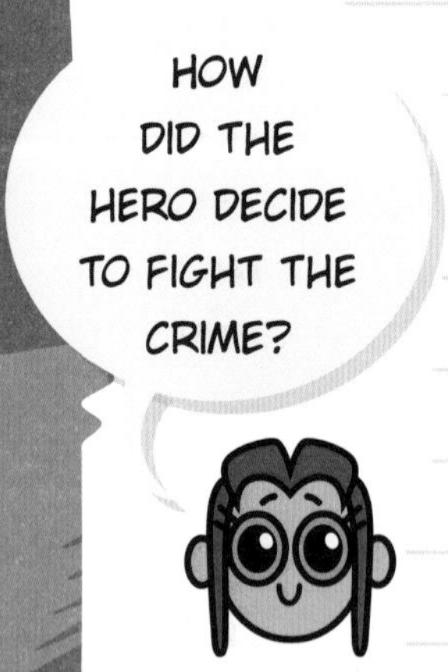
HOW DID THE HERO DECIDE TO FIGHT THE CRIME?

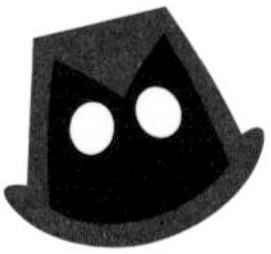

HAVE SOMEBODY FIND OUT YOUR HERO'S WEAKNESS.

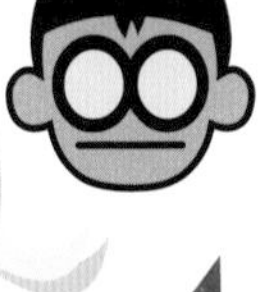

BUT THE HERO OVERCOMES IT ALL AND SAVES THE DAY!

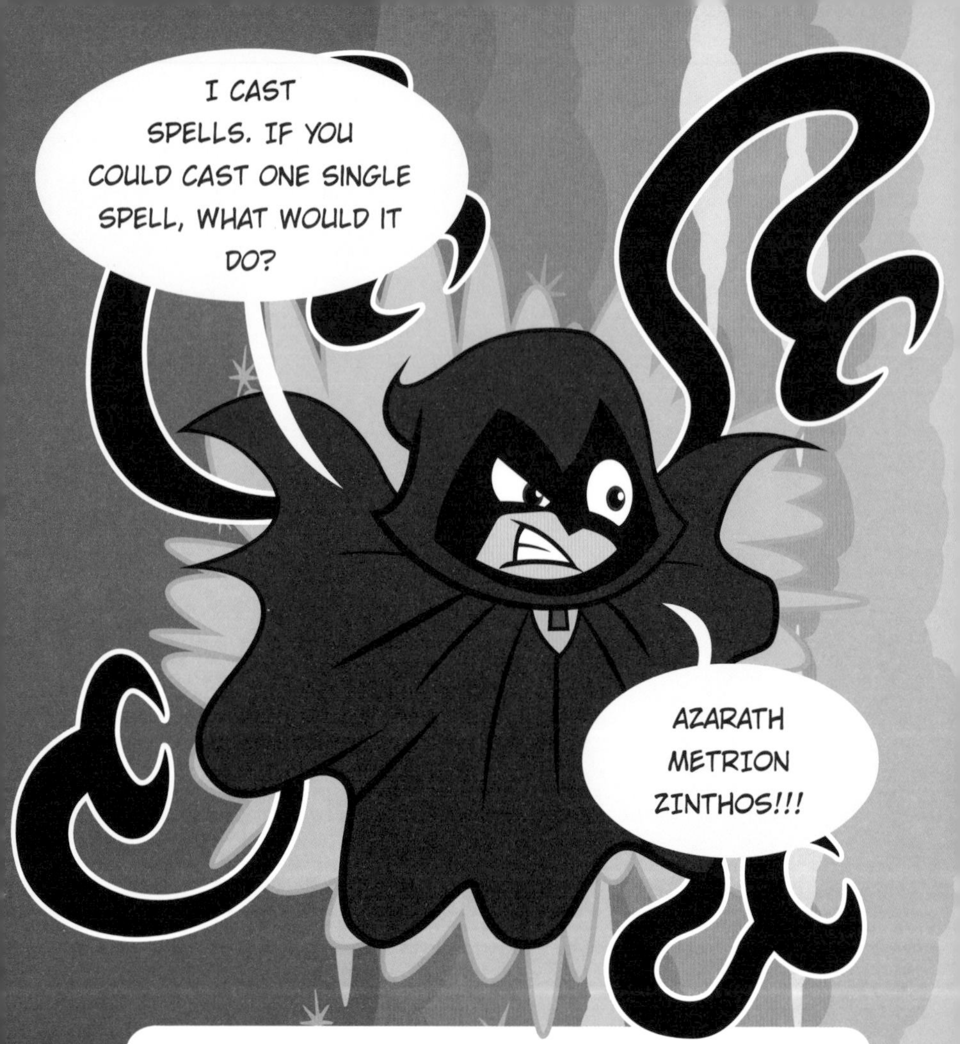
I CAST SPELLS. IF YOU COULD CAST ONE SINGLE SPELL, WHAT WOULD IT DO?
AZARATH METRION ZINTHOS!!!

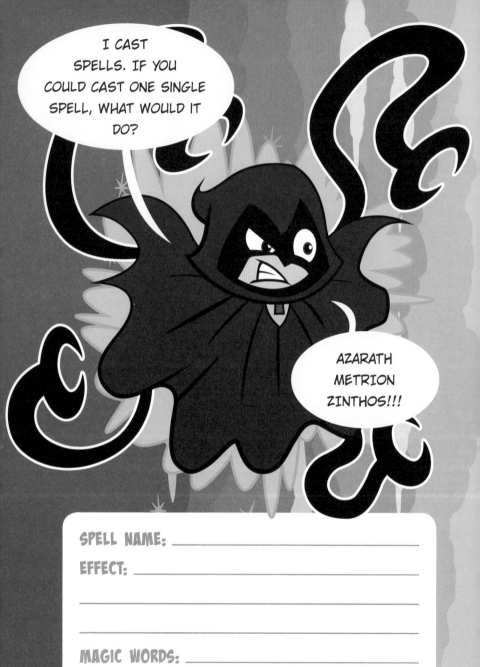

SPELL NAME: ______________________________

EFFECT: ______________________________

____

____

MAGIC WORDS: ______________________________

____

Complete the story by filling in the words. Make the story correct or make it silly!

A power move is when one super hero takes a power and combines it with the ______________ (NOUN) of another super hero to ______________ (VERB) a brand-new ______________ (NOUN). For example, there is the Power Ball Shuffle where Beast Boy turns into a/an ______________ (ANIMAL) and ______________ (PERSON IN ROOM) squirts his ______________ (TYPE OF LIQUID) at a bad guy! Then, there's the Thunder Alley ______________ (NOUN) where Beast Boy turns into a/an ______________ (ADJECTIVE) gorilla and throws Cyborg's ______________ (PART OF THE BODY) at the baddie. Watch out for the Power Rang, too. That's when Robin throws his ______________ (NOUN) and

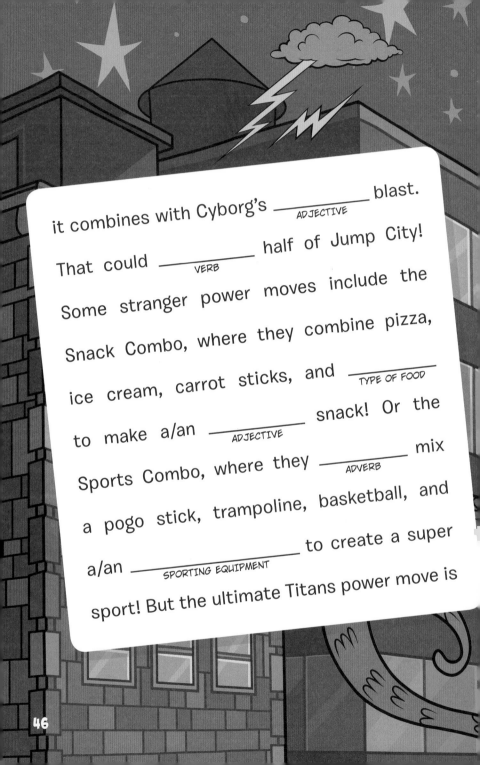

it combines with Cyborg's _____ blast.
ADJECTIVE

That could _____ half of Jump City!
VERB

Some stranger power moves include the

Snack Combo, where they combine pizza,

ice cream, carrot sticks, and _____
TYPE OF FOOD

to make a/an _____ snack! Or the
ADJECTIVE

Sports Combo, where they _____ mix
ADVERB

a pogo stick, trampoline, basketball, and

a/an _____ to create a super
SPORTING EQUIPMENT

sport! But the ultimate Titans power move is

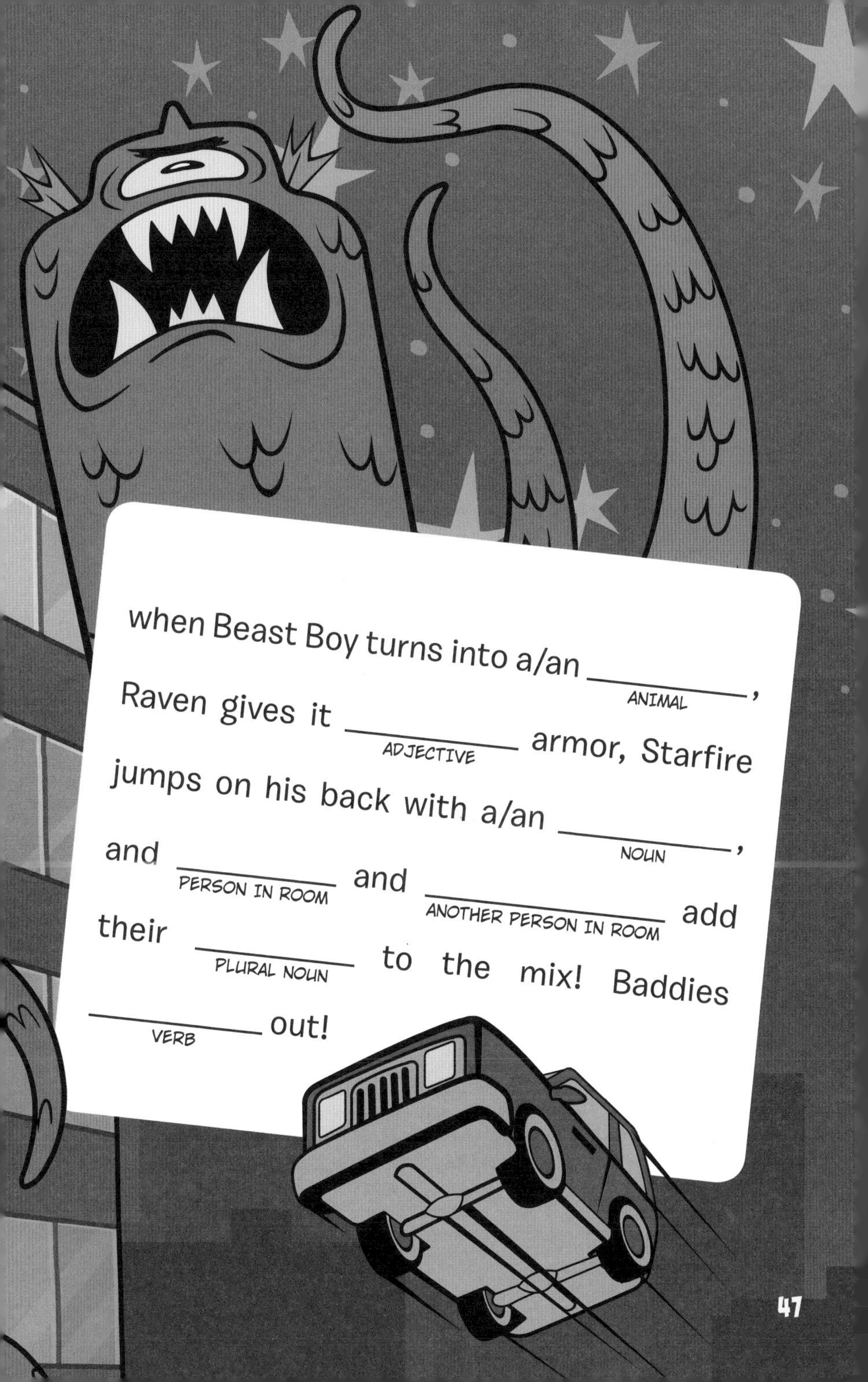

when Beast Boy turns into a/an ____________,
ANIMAL

Raven gives it ____________ armor, Starfire
ADJECTIVE

jumps on his back with a/an ____________,
NOUN

and ____________ and ____________ add
PERSON IN ROOM / ANOTHER PERSON IN ROOM

their ____________ to the mix! Baddies
PLURAL NOUN

____________ out!
VERB

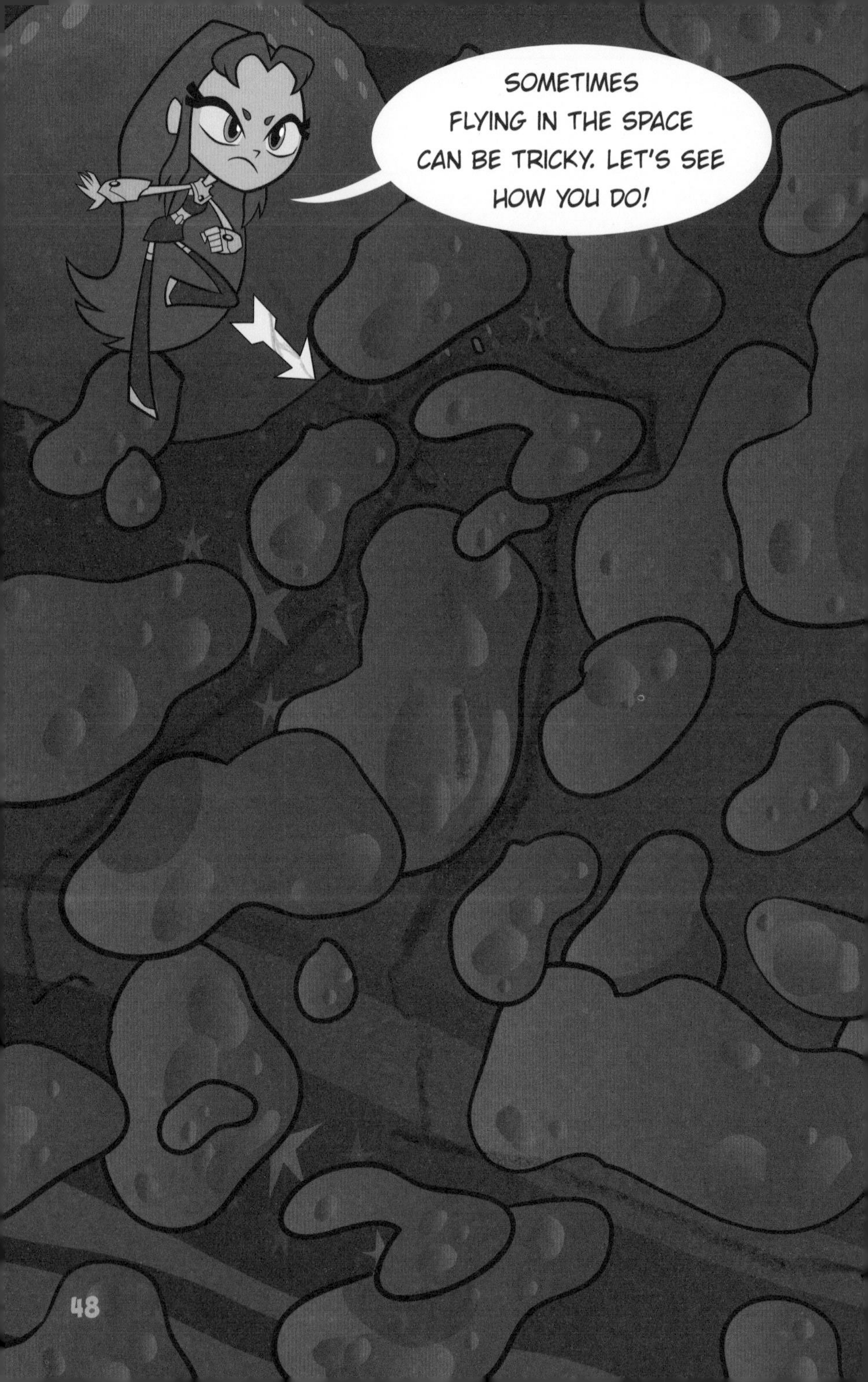
SOMETIMES FLYING IN THE SPACE CAN BE TRICKY. LET'S SEE HOW YOU DO!

Hold your pen at the very end with only two fingers, and place the tip on the top arrow. Try to guide it to Earth without hitting an asteroid!

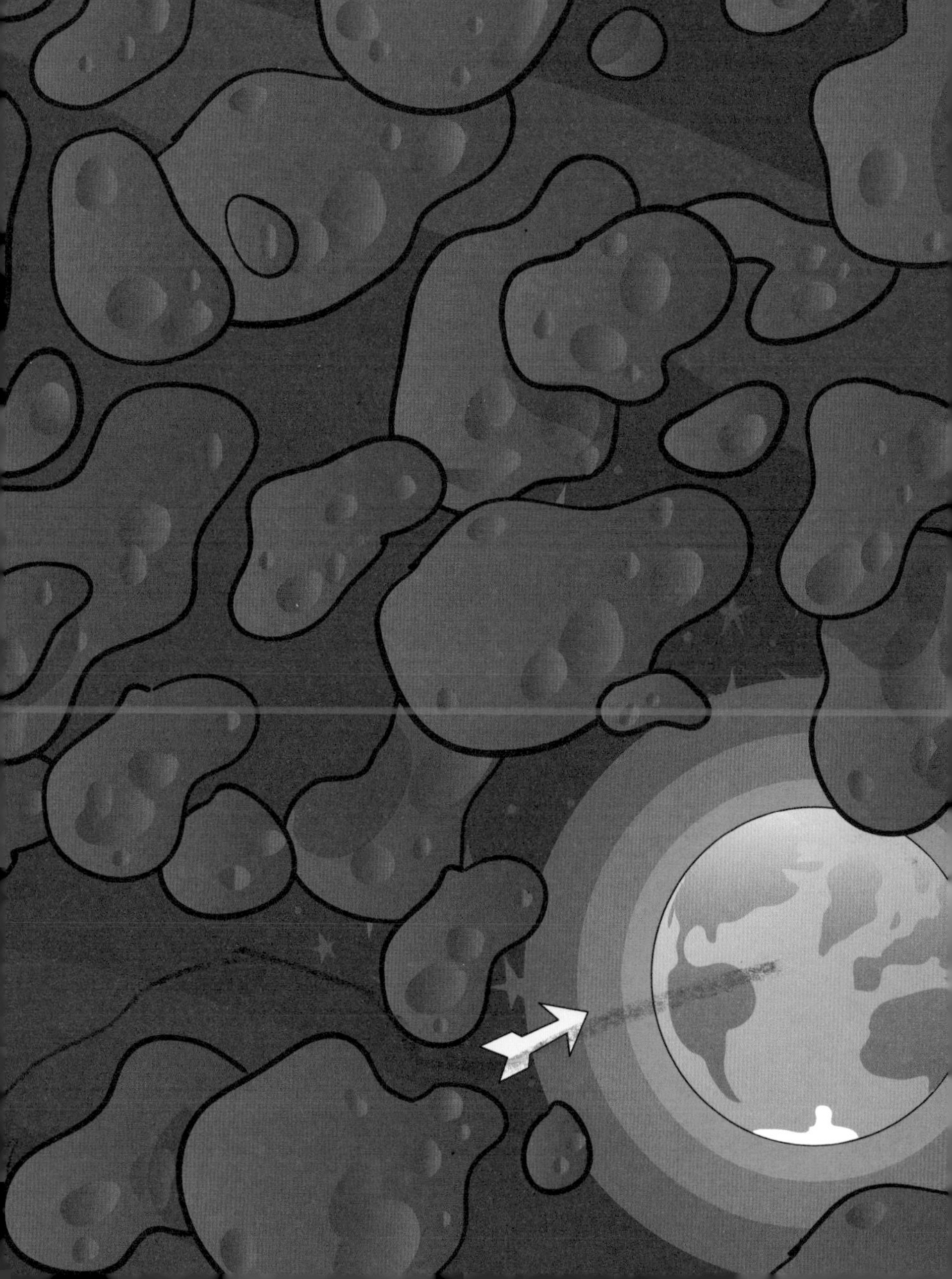

Robin learned his acrobatic skills growing up in the circus. If you worked in the circus, what would you want to be?

ACROBAT
CLOWN
LION TAMER
TICKET SALESPERSON
HUMAN CANNONBALL
TRAPEZE ARTIST
TIGHTROPE WALKER
DAREDEVIL
SWORD SWALLOWER
POOP SCOOPER
RINGMASTER
ELEPHANT

OTHER: _____

WHAT WOULD YOU CHOOSE FOR A CIRCUS STAGE NAME?

_____

The Titans once had a hot-dog-eating contest. List your three favorite foods. Could you eat only those foods for the rest of your life?

1. _____

_____

2. _____

_____

3. _____

_____

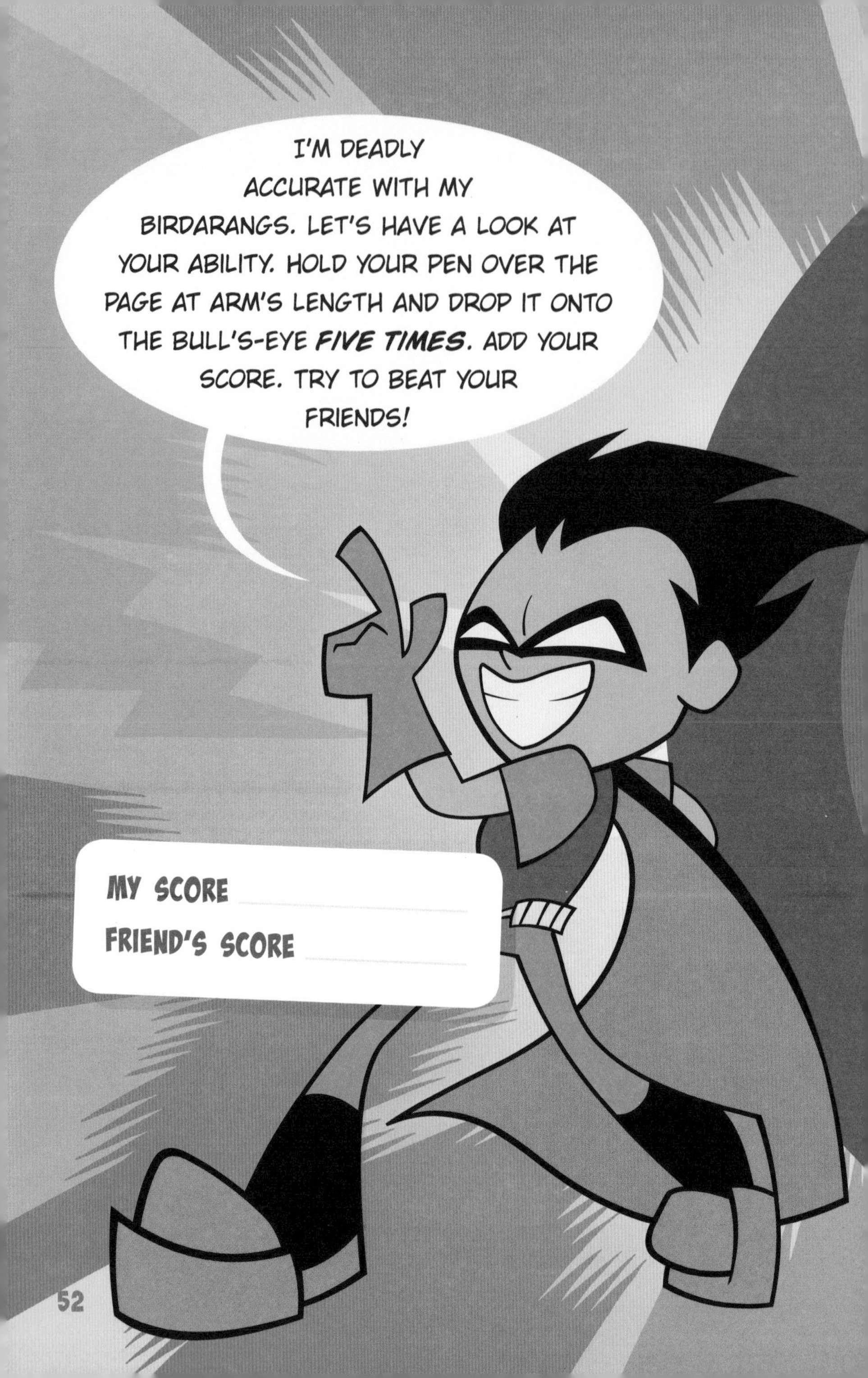
I'M DEADLY ACCURATE WITH MY BIRDARANGS. LET'S HAVE A LOOK AT YOUR ABILITY. HOLD YOUR PEN OVER THE PAGE AT ARM'S LENGTH AND DROP IT ONTO THE BULL'S-EYE *FIVE TIMES*. ADD YOUR SCORE. TRY TO BEAT YOUR FRIENDS!
MY SCORE ____________
FRIEND'S SCORE ____________

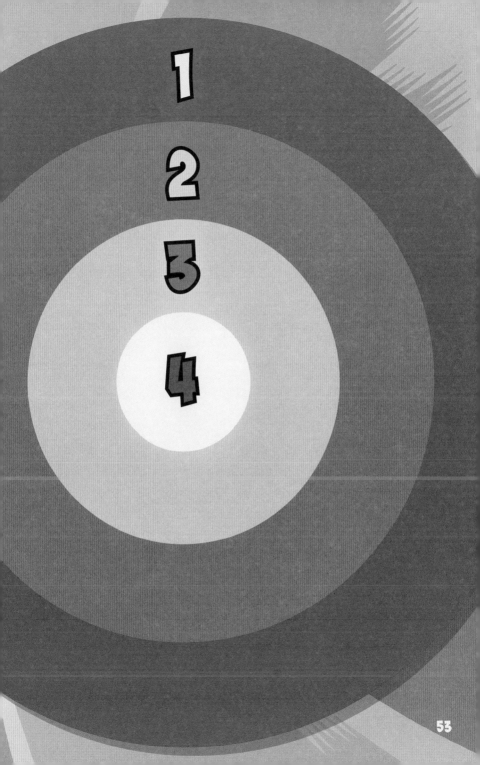

1

2

3

4

The Teen Titans once used bees as money. What would happen if we used bees as money? What about flowers? Seeds? Rocks? If you could make up your own kind of money, what would it be like?

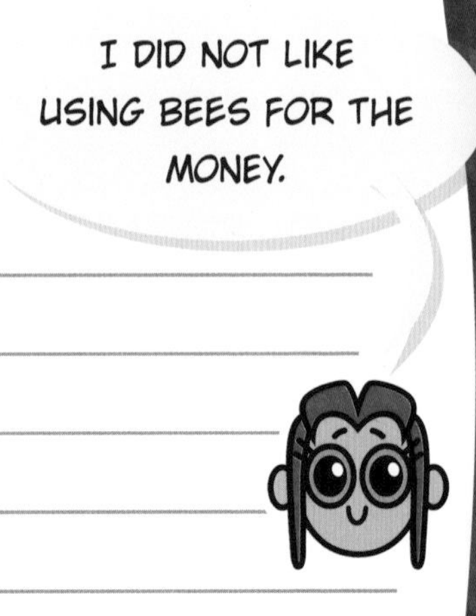
I DID NOT LIKE USING BEES FOR THE MONEY.

Sometimes the Titans use the game Rock-Paper-Scissors to solve a conflict.

PAPER BEATS ROCK.
SCISSORS BEAT PAPER.
ROCK BEATS SCISSORS.

Think of your own game of Rock-Paper-Scissors, using different items. Invent hand signals for each one. Now, try to play it with a friend!

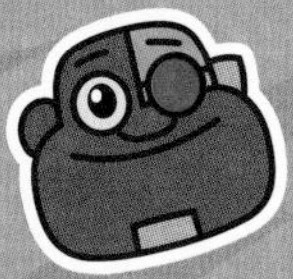
I LIKE ROCKET-RUST-OIL!

ITEM: ____________________

HAND SIGNAL: ____________________

____

ITEM: ____________________

HAND SIGNAL: ____________________

____

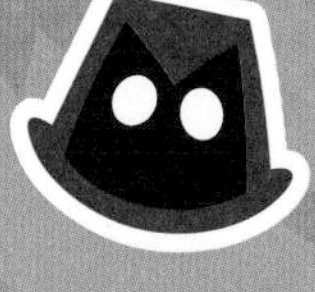
THIS IS BORING, BORING, BORING.

ITEM: ____________________

HAND SIGNAL: ____________________

____

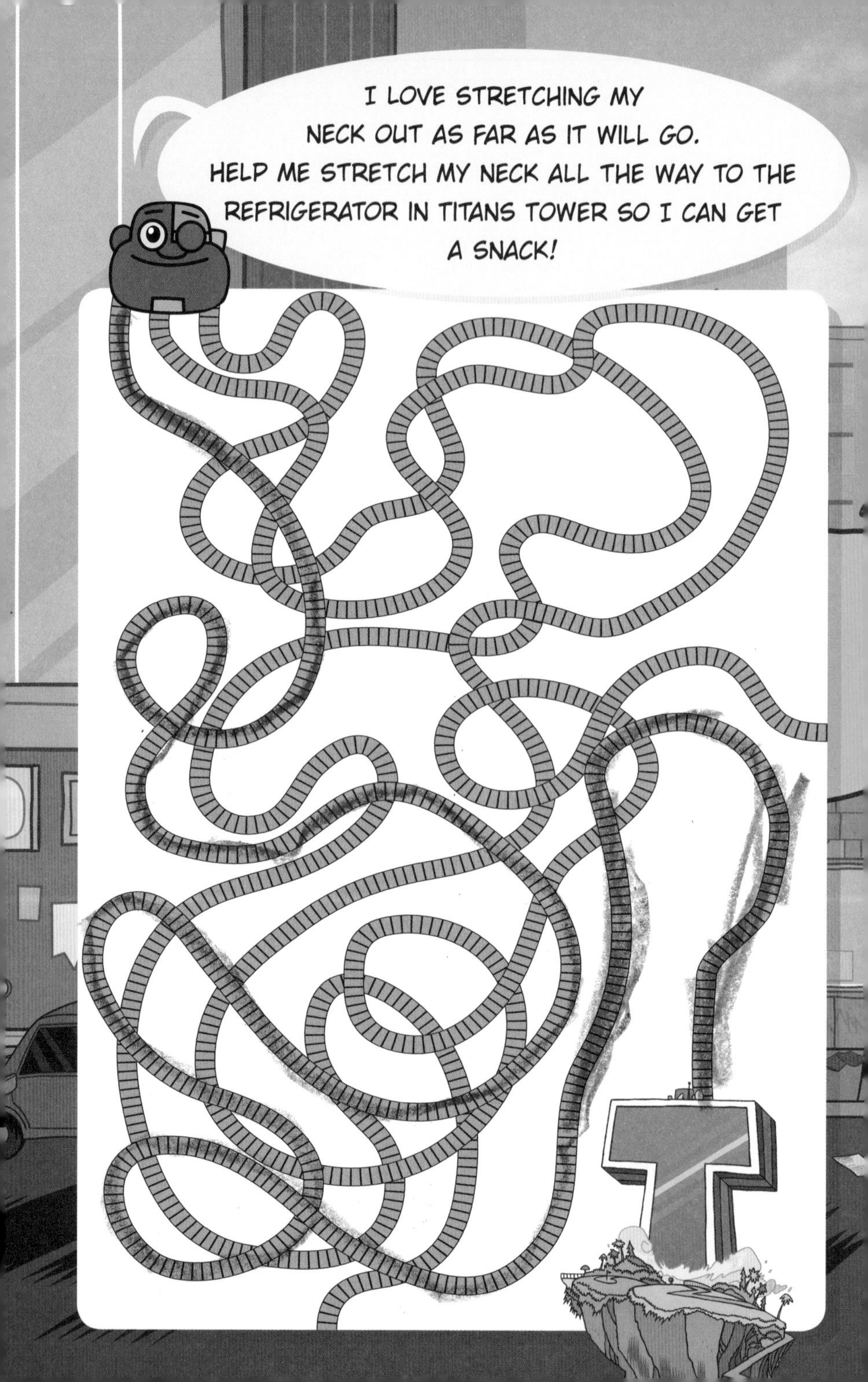
I LOVE STRETCHING MY NECK OUT AS FAR AS IT WILL GO. HELP ME STRETCH MY NECK ALL THE WAY TO THE REFRIGERATOR IN TITANS TOWER SO I CAN GET A SNACK!

MATCHING TIME!

Match all the villains of H.I.V.E. Five with their special abilities:

BODY MULTIPLICATION

INCREDIBLE STRENGTH

TECHNOLOGICAL GENIUS

AWESOME VISION AND EYE BLASTS

CURSING OBJECTS AND HEX BLAST

GIZMO

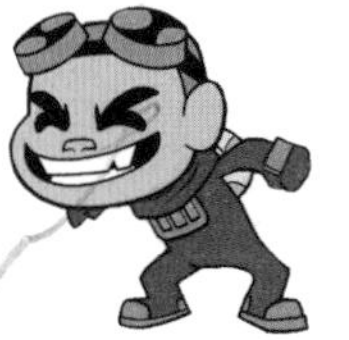

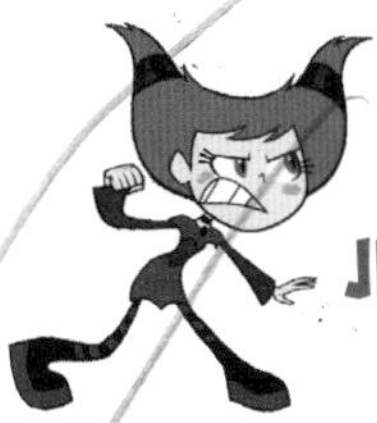

JINX

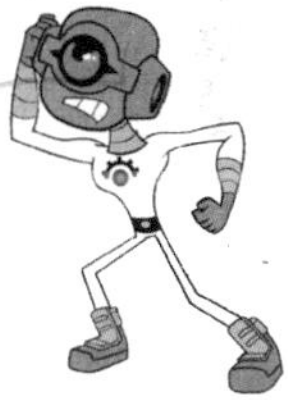

SEE-MORE

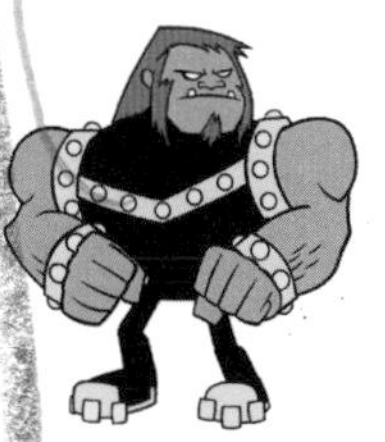

MAMMOTH

BILLY NUMEROUS

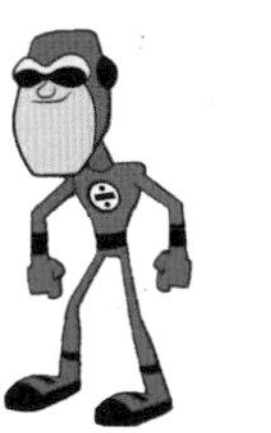

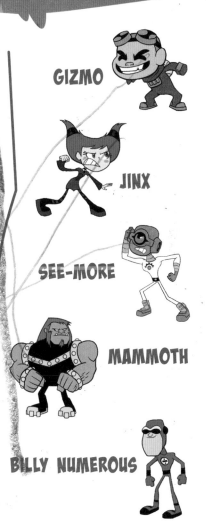

SOMETIMES THE TITANS LIKE TO GO ON A BOYS' OR GIRLS' NIGHT OUT. IF YOU WERE GOING ON THE PERFECT NIGHT OUT, WHAT WOULD IT INCLUDE?

PAR-TAYYYYY!!!!!

CITY: _____

CONCERT: _____

CELEBRITY WITH YOU: _____

RESTAURANT: _____

AWESOME RIDE: _____

CRAZY OUTFIT: _____

HAT: _____

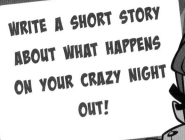

WRITE A SHORT STORY ABOUT WHAT HAPPENS ON YOUR CRAZY NIGHT OUT!

I HOPE IT DOES NOT INCLUDE A VISIT FROM THE OFFICERS OF THE POLICE.

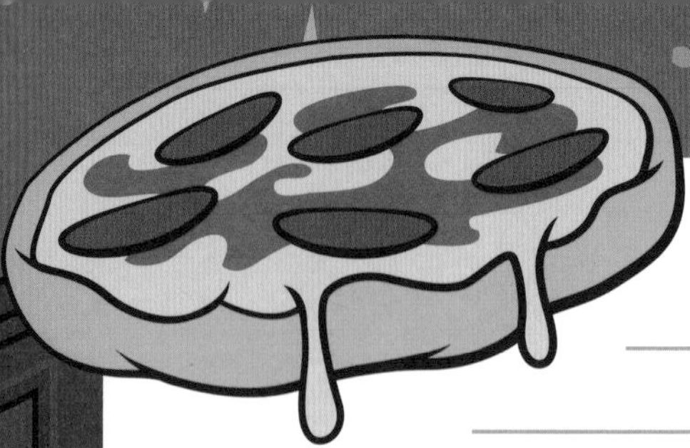

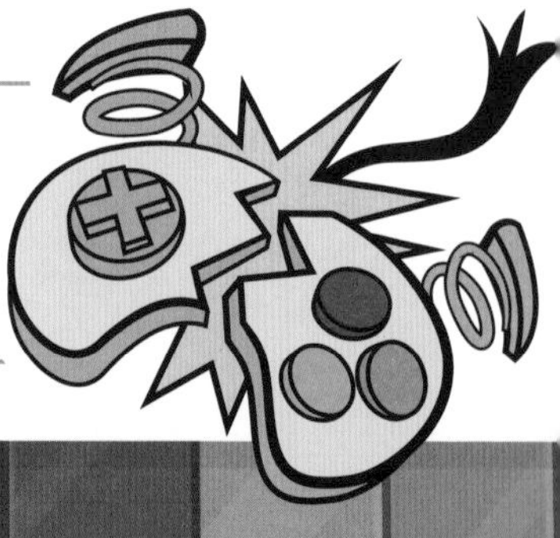

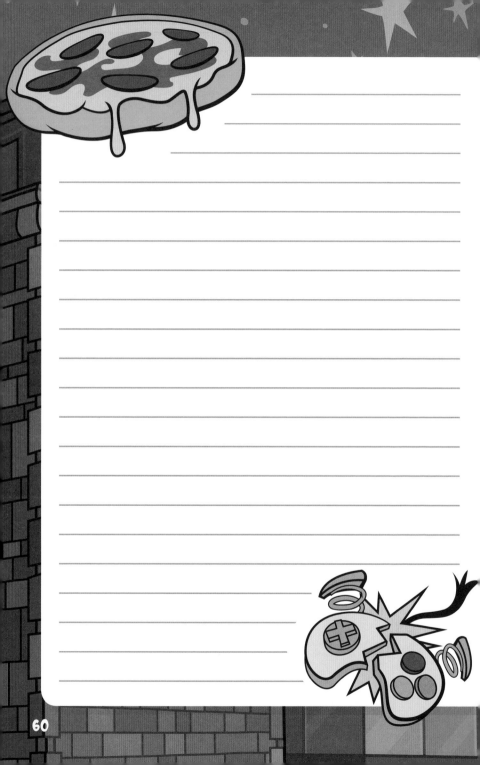

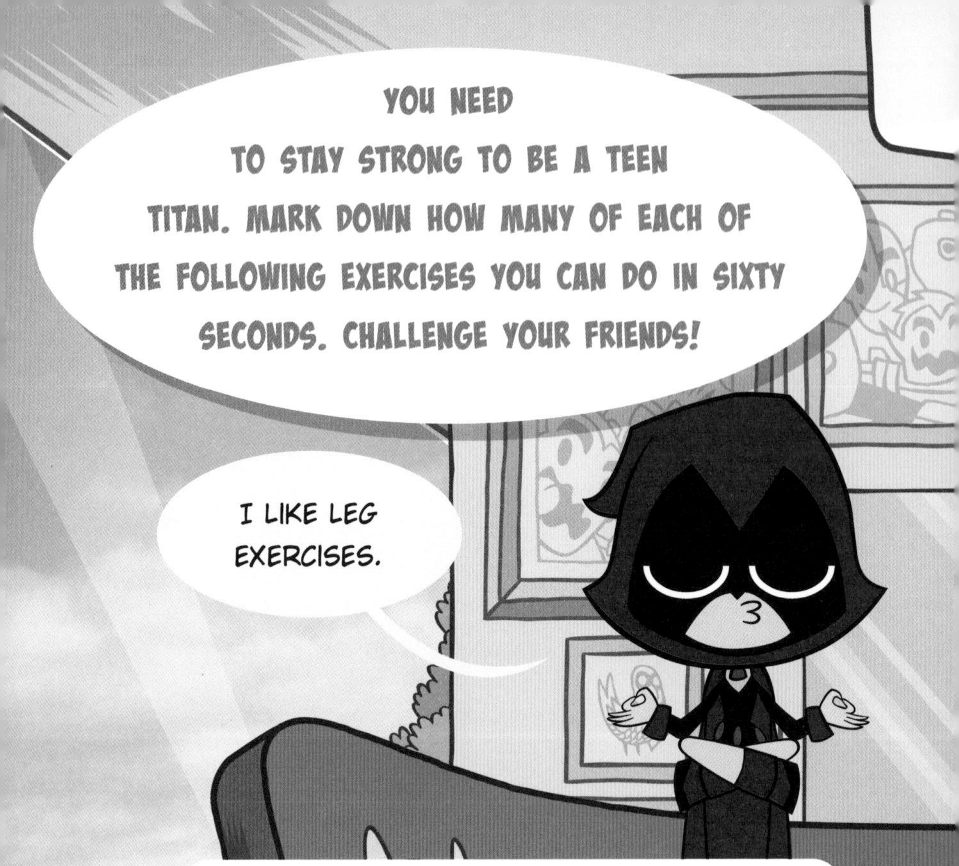
YOU NEED TO STAY STRONG TO BE A TEEN TITAN. MARK DOWN HOW MANY OF EACH OF THE FOLLOWING EXERCISES YOU CAN DO IN SIXTY SECONDS. CHALLENGE YOUR FRIENDS!
I LIKE LEG EXERCISES.

PUSH-UPS: ______________________

SIT-UPS: ______________________

JUMPING JACKS: ______________________

LOW SQUAT JUMPS: ______________________

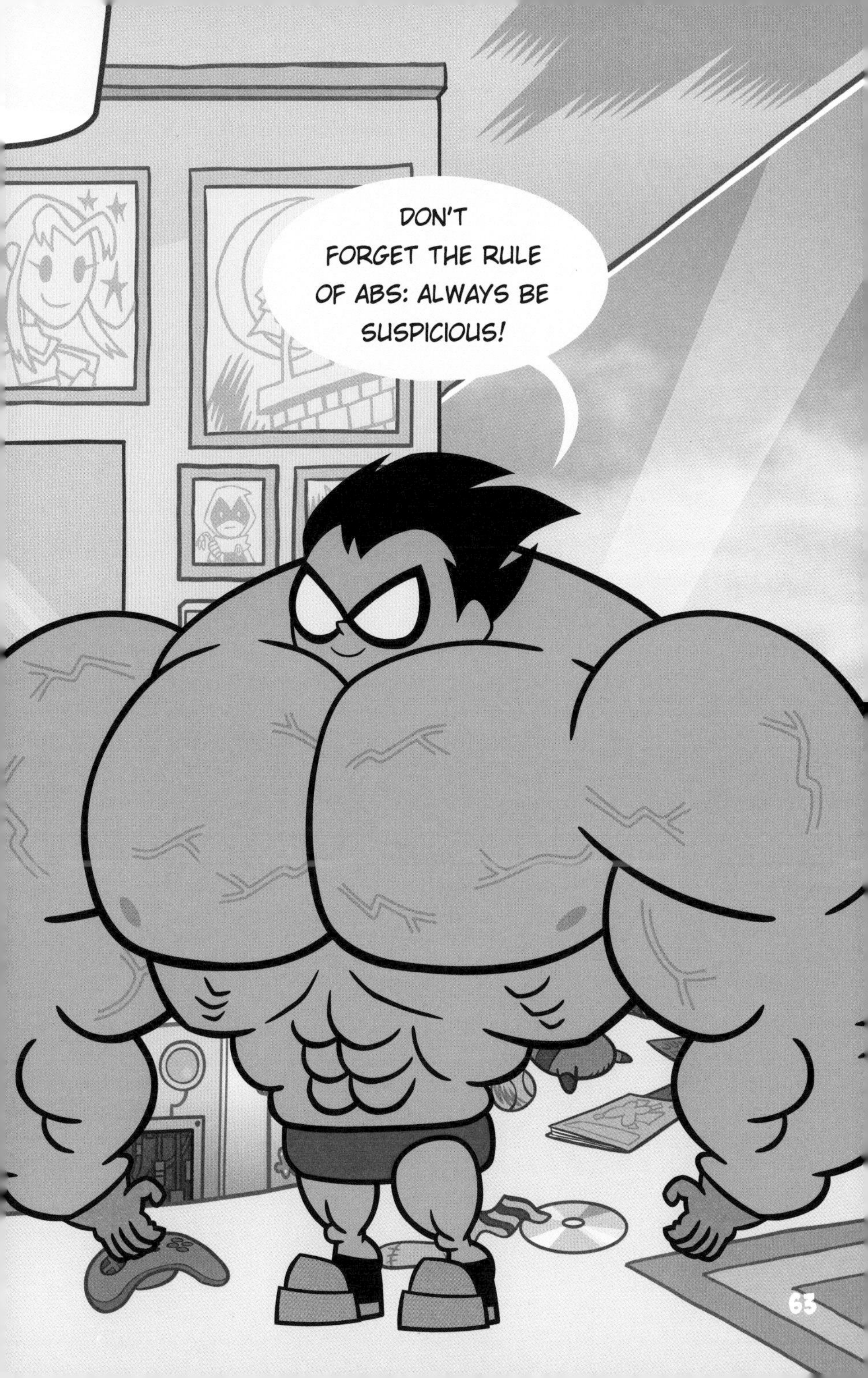
DON'T FORGET THE RULE OF ABS: ALWAYS BE SUSPICIOUS!

Titans Tower looks like a giant letter T. If you could have your house look like a giant letter, which would you pick and why? Draw your tower and label where all the rooms should go. Then give it a name!

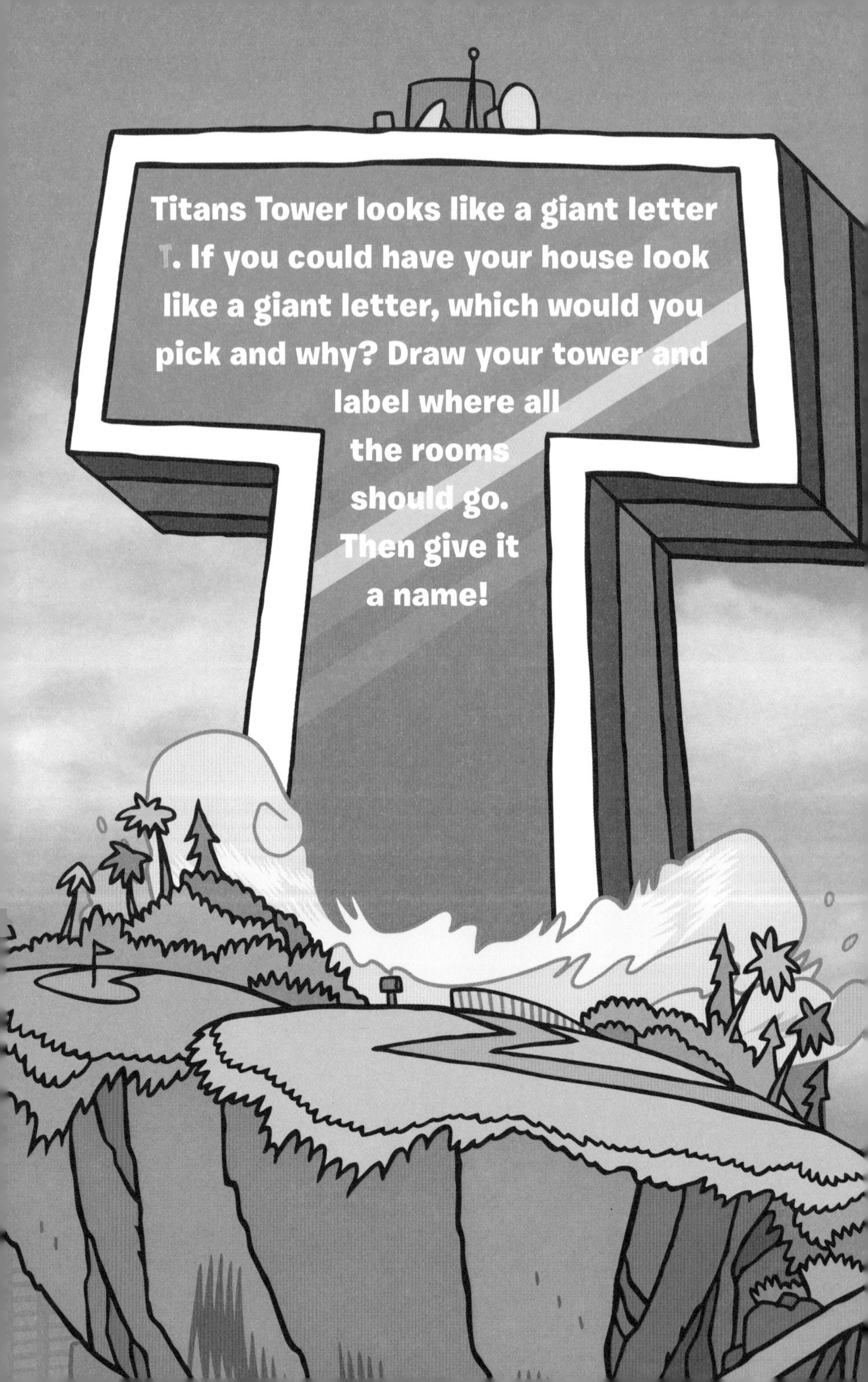

MOTHER MAE-EYE IS A MEAN OLD SUPER-VILLAIN WHO WE ONCE FACED. SHE HAD SPECIAL MOVES CALLED THE PURSE PUNCH AND THE FINGER WAG.

WHAT SPECIAL MOVES WOULD YOUR FAMILY MEMBERS HAVE IF THEY WERE SUPERPOWERED BADDIES?

NAME: _____

VILLAIN POWERS: _____

_____

NAME: _____

VILLAIN POWERS: _____

_____

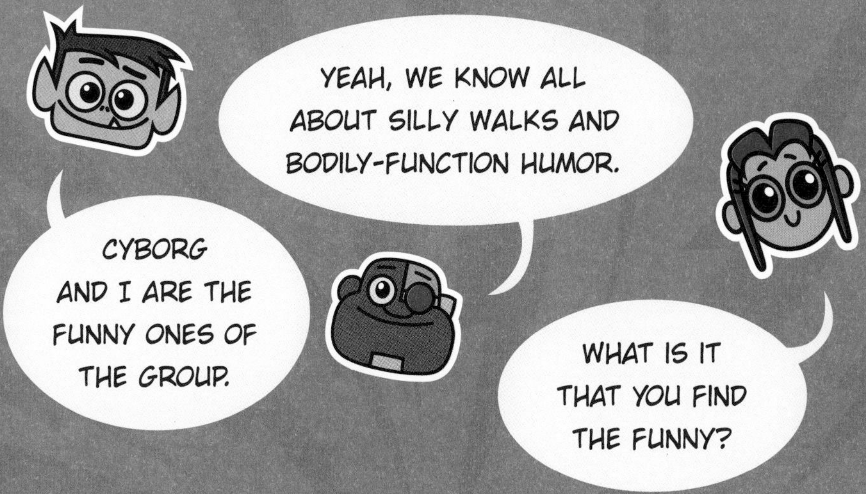
CYBORG AND I ARE THE FUNNY ONES OF THE GROUP.
YEAH, WE KNOW ALL ABOUT SILLY WALKS AND BODILY-FUNCTION HUMOR.
WHAT IS IT THAT YOU FIND THE FUNNY?

WHAT WAS THE FUNNIEST THING THAT EVER HAPPENED TO YOU OR A FRIEND?

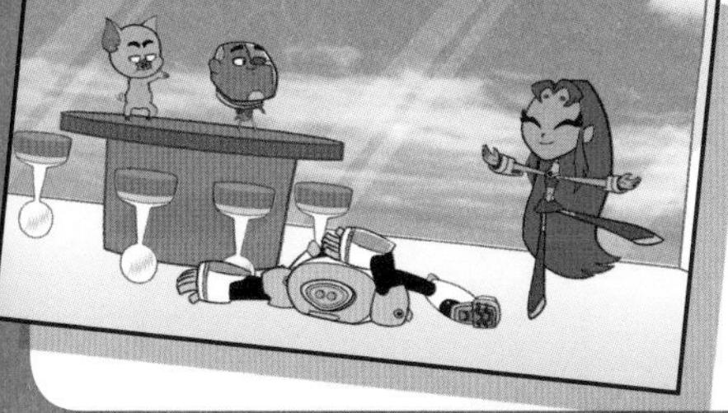

Silkie has terrible nightmares.
Describe your WORST nightmare.

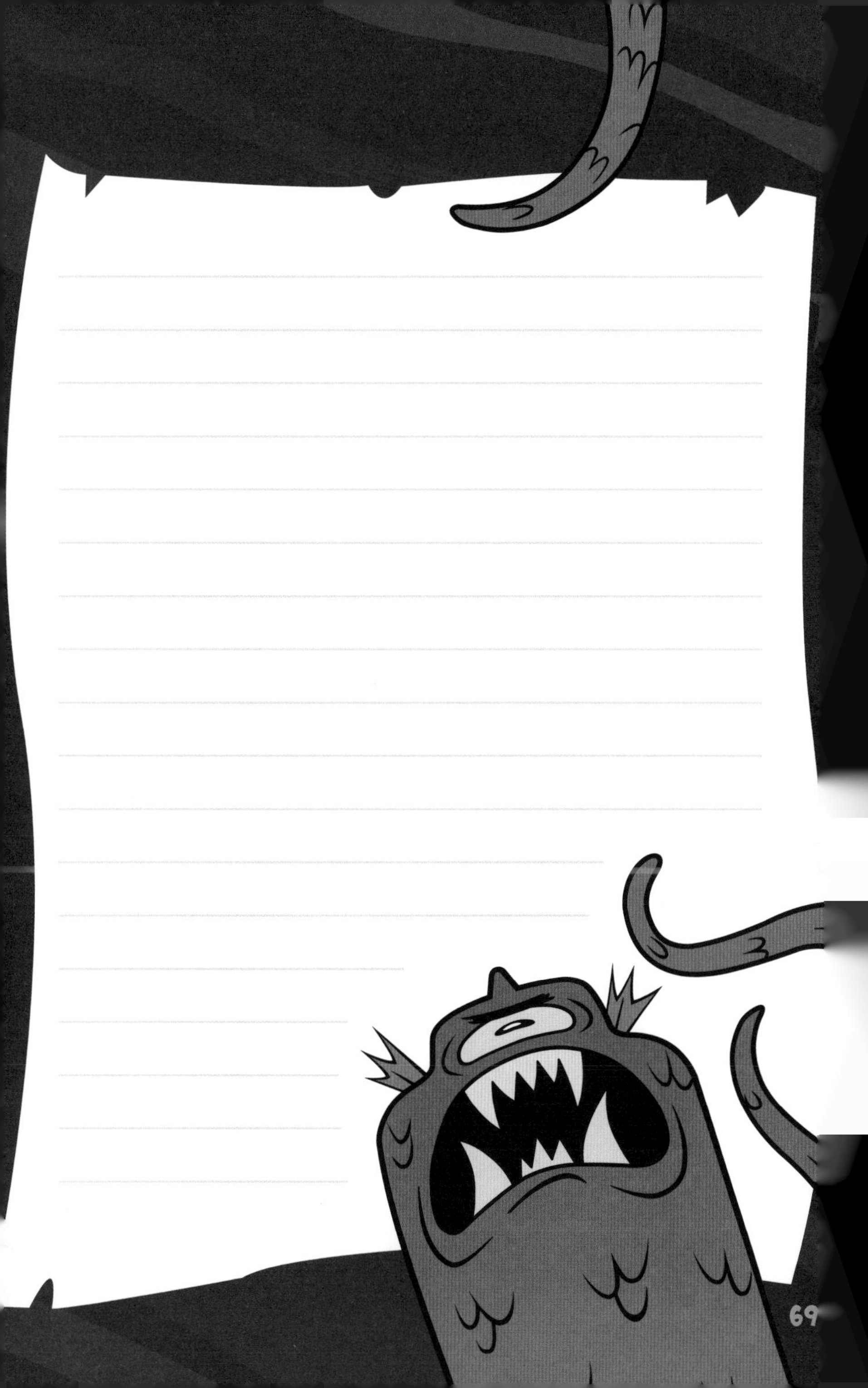

EVERY SUPER HERO HAS A SPECIAL HEROIC POSE.
MAKE UP POSES FOR THE FOLLOWING SUPER HEROES:

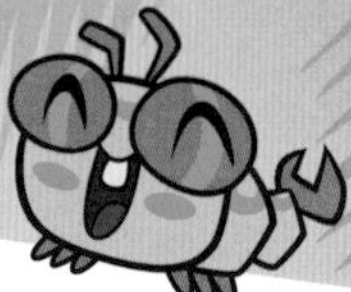

ROBIN: One knee up at a ninety-degree angle, shoulders back, facing into the wind

RAVEN:

STARFIRE:

CYBORG:

BEAST BOY:

SILKIE:

BUMBLEBEE:

SPEEDY:

AQUALAD:

MAS:

MENOS:

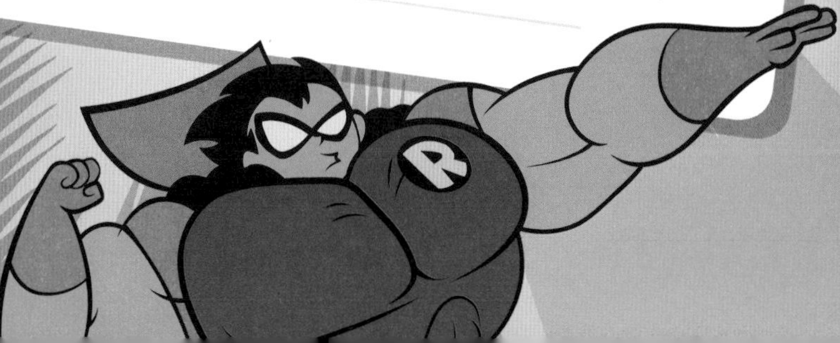

Cyborg can program his dreams by launching his brain into Dream Mode. If you could pick your dreams, describe the one you would have MOST OFTEN!

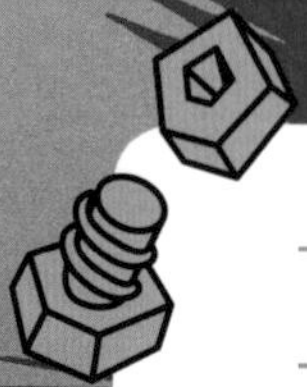

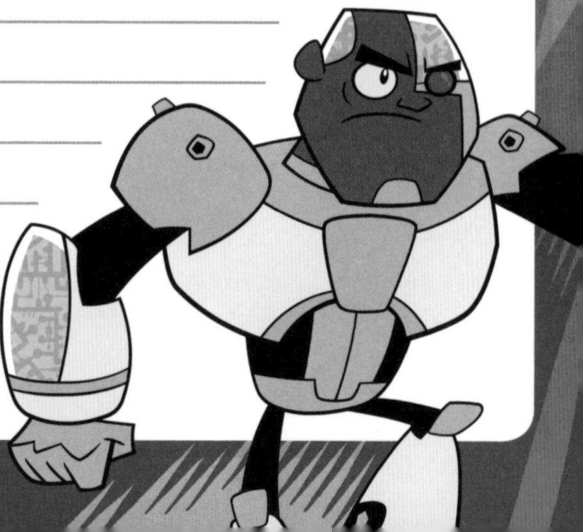

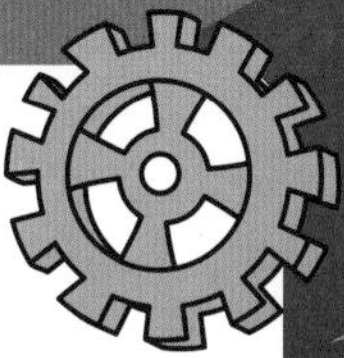

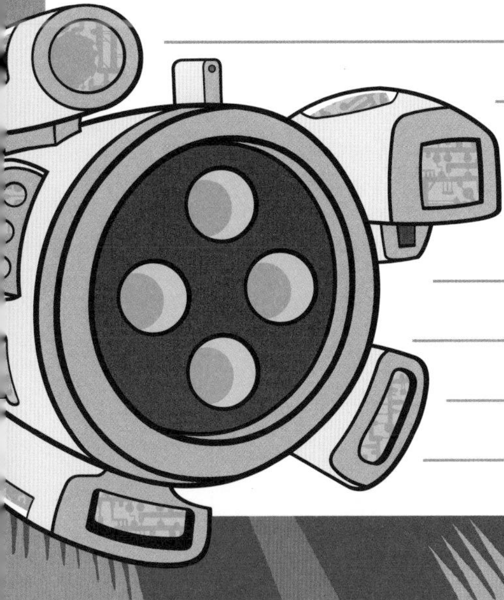

MANY SUPER HEROES ARE CREATED BY FREAKY, HORRIBLE ACCIDENTS. IF ROBIN MERGED HIS DNA WITH AN ACTUAL ROBIN, WHAT POWERS MIGHT HE GET? THINK OF FIVE!

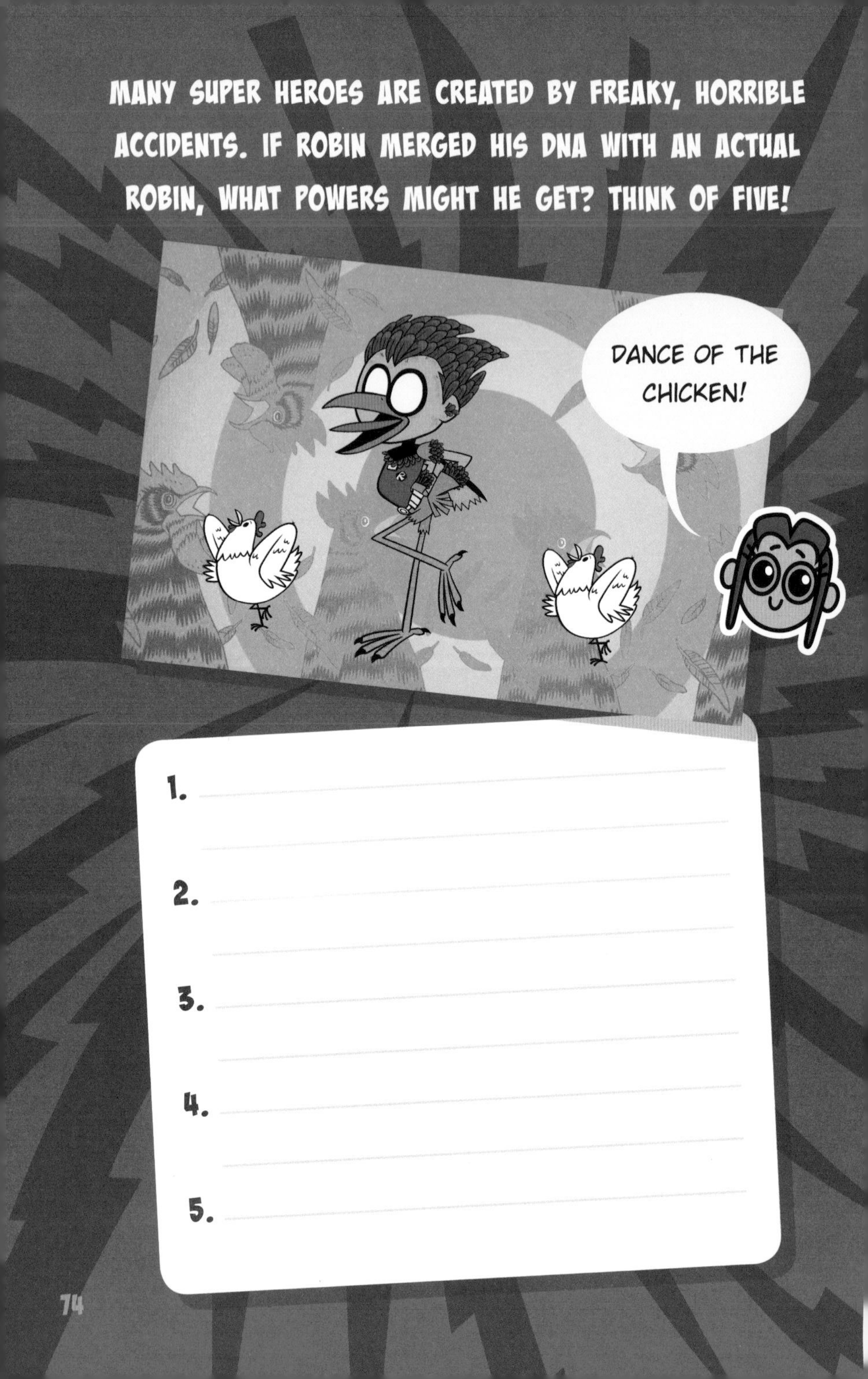
DANCE OF THE CHICKEN!

1. ____________________

2. ____________________

3. ____________________

4. ____________________

5. ____________________

WHEN THE TITANS ARE OFF ON AN ADVENTURE, SILKIE STAYS BEHIND TO GUARD TITANS TOWER. WRITE A STORY ABOUT SILKIE DEFENDING THE TOWER AGAINST THE H.I.V.E. FIVE!

_____

_____
_____
_____
_____
_____
_____
_____

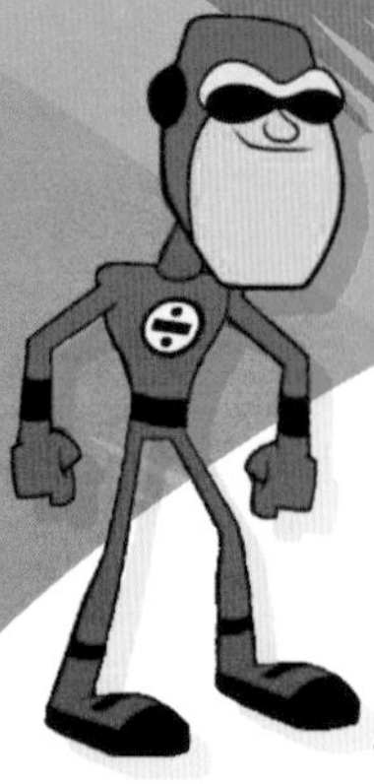

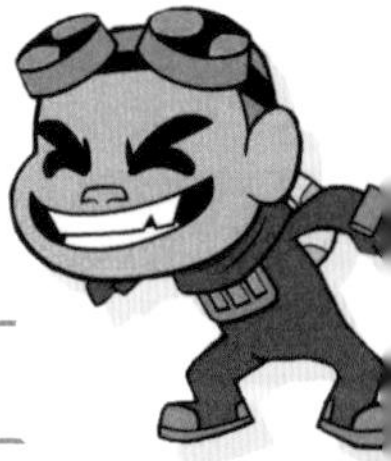

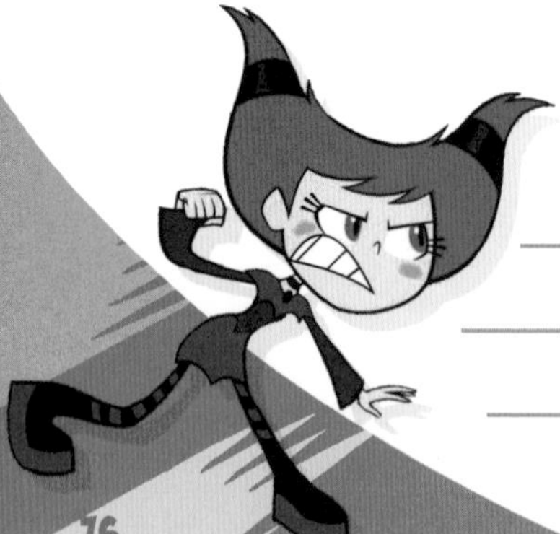

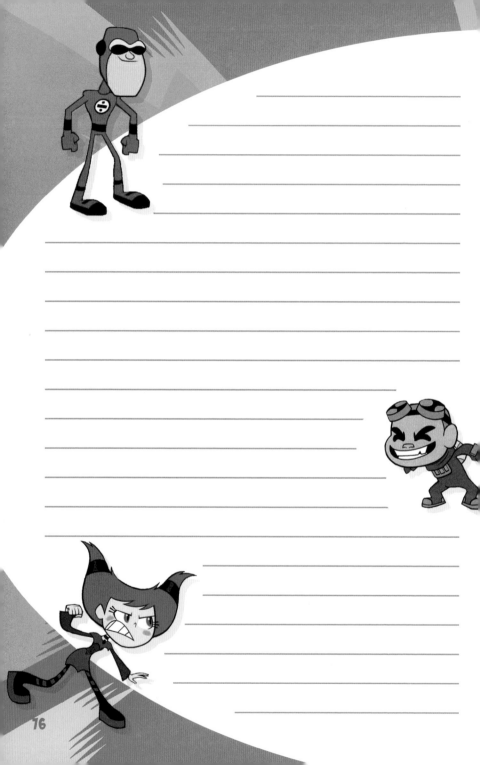

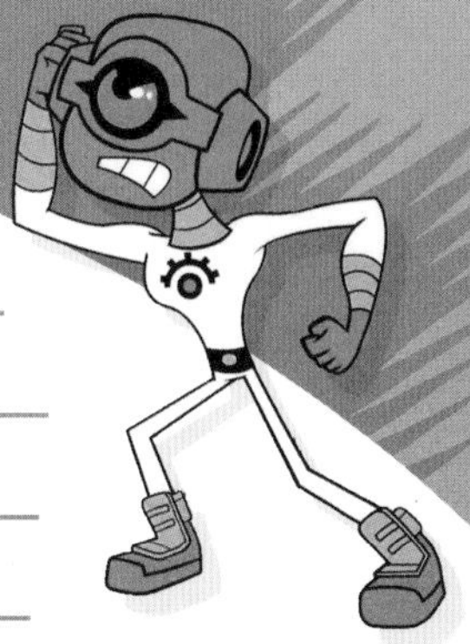

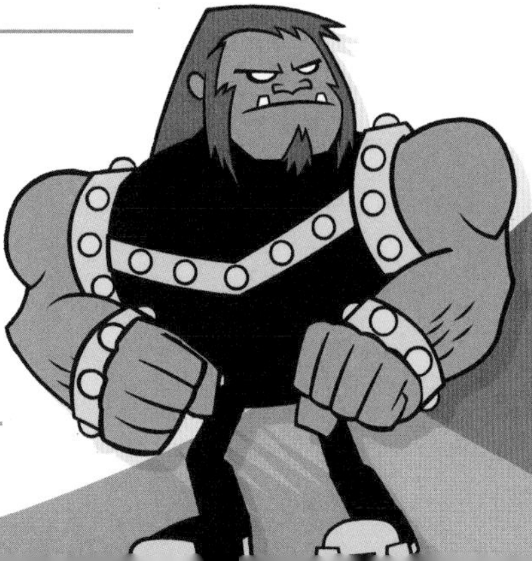

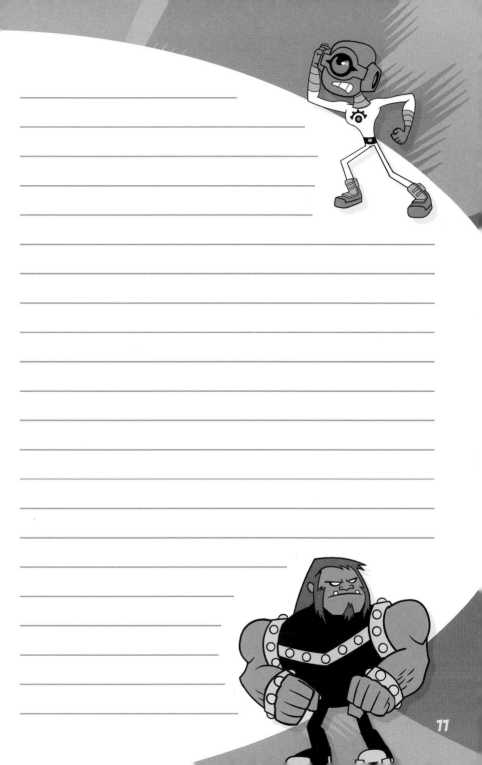

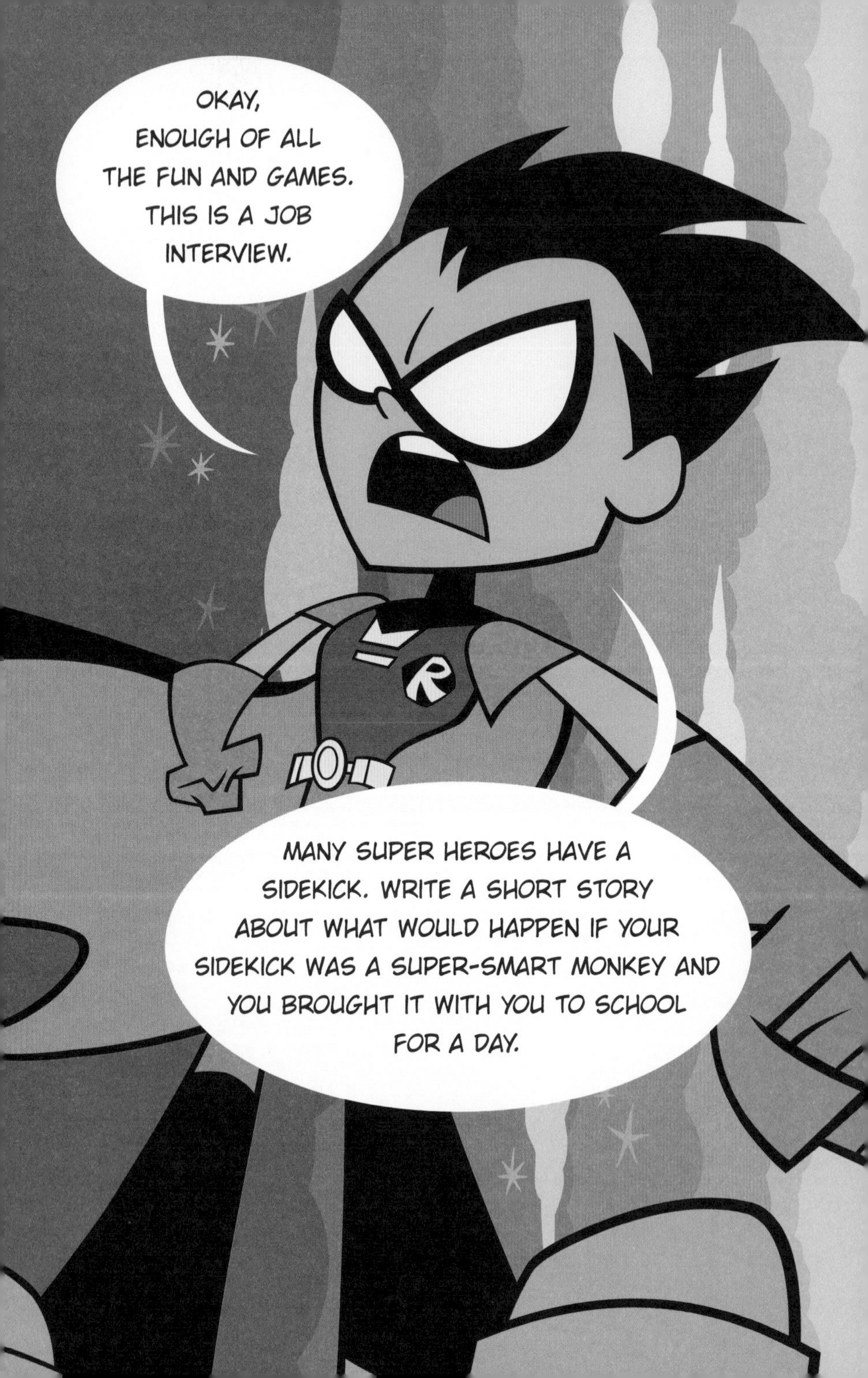
OKAY, ENOUGH OF ALL THE FUN AND GAMES. THIS IS A JOB INTERVIEW.
MANY SUPER HEROES HAVE A SIDEKICK. WRITE A SHORT STORY ABOUT WHAT WOULD HAPPEN IF YOUR SIDEKICK WAS A SUPER-SMART MONKEY AND YOU BROUGHT IT WITH YOU TO SCHOOL FOR A DAY.

ANOTHER INTERVIEW QUESTION. IF YOU COULD BE BEST IN THE WORLD AT FIVE THINGS, WHAT WOULD THEY BE?

1.
2.
3.
4.
5.

WHAT WOULD YOU DO WITH YOUR SWEET SKILLS?

82

AND A FEW OTHER QUESTIONS:

WOULD YOU RATHER . . .

Have the power of flight OR the power of super speed?

Have Raven's powers OR Beast Boy's powers?

Fly to outer space OR discover a treasure under the sea?

Be an average sidekick OR an evil mastermind?

Live in Titans Tower OR have your dream job someplace else?

Have a cool hero costume OR a theme song?

ASK YOUR FRIENDS!

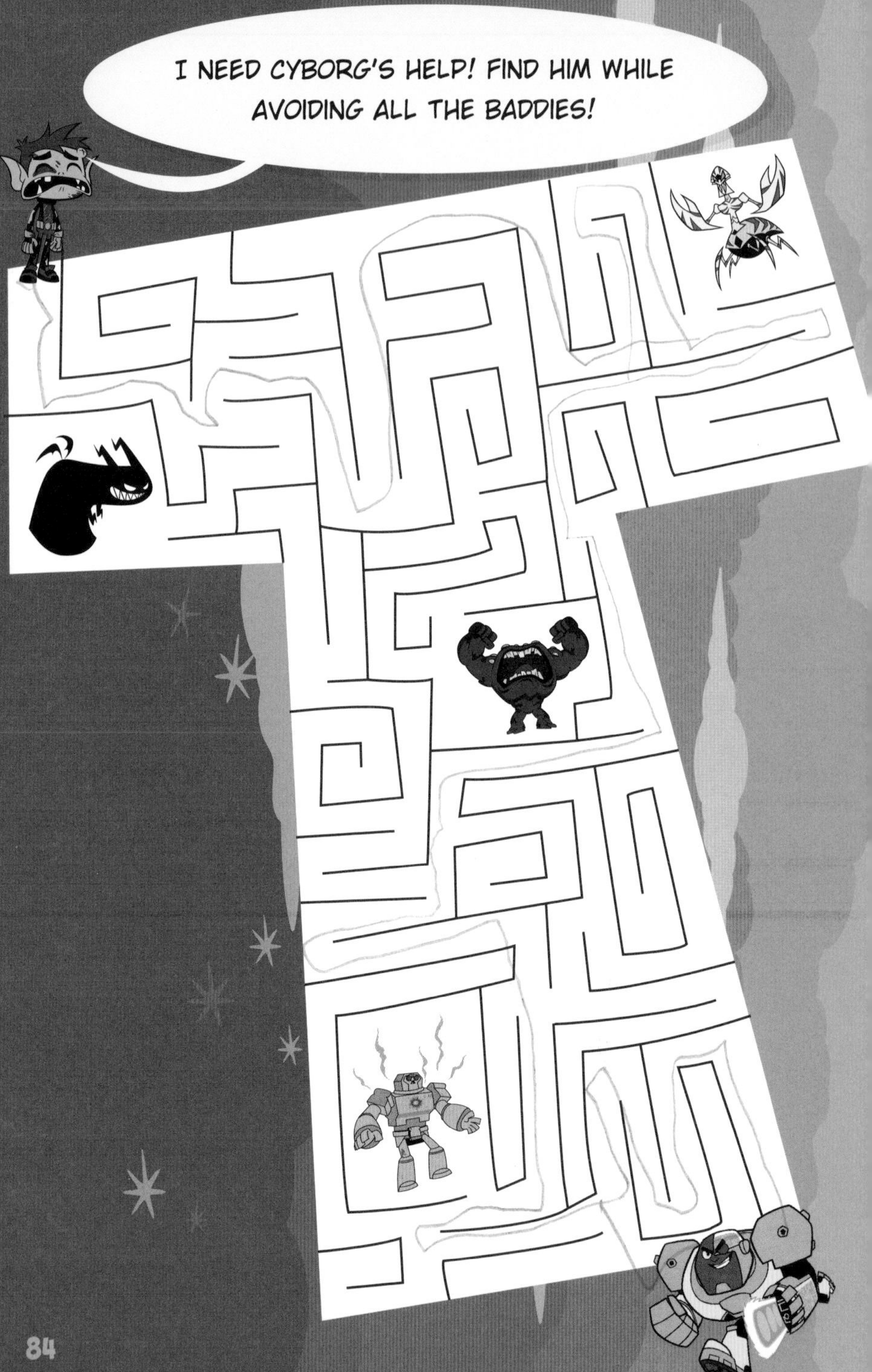
I NEED CYBORG'S HELP! FIND HIM WHILE AVOIDING ALL THE BADDIES!

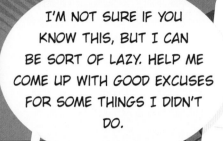

I'M NOT SURE IF YOU KNOW THIS, BUT I CAN BE SORT OF LAZY. HELP ME COME UP WITH GOOD EXCUSES FOR SOME THINGS I DIDN'T DO.

Why I didn't clean up the Tower when it was my turn:

Why I ate Beast Boy's sandwich from the fridge:

Why I didn't brush my teeth:

Why I "forgot" to walk Silkie:

Why I didn't respond to Robin's distress call:

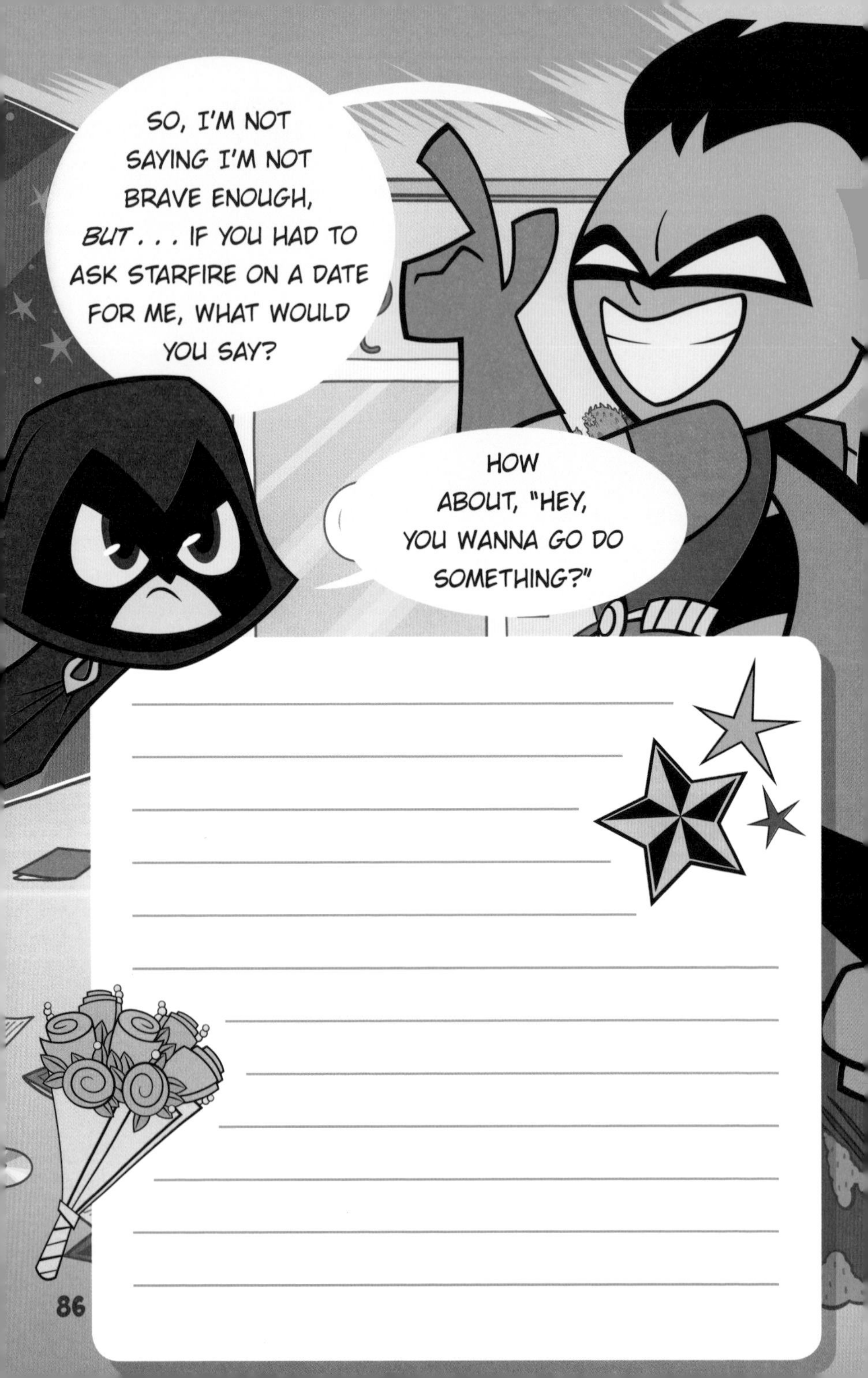
SO, I'M NOT SAYING I'M NOT BRAVE ENOUGH, *BUT* . . . IF YOU HAD TO ASK STARFIRE ON A DATE FOR ME, WHAT WOULD YOU SAY?
HOW ABOUT, "HEY, YOU WANNA GO DO SOMETHING?"

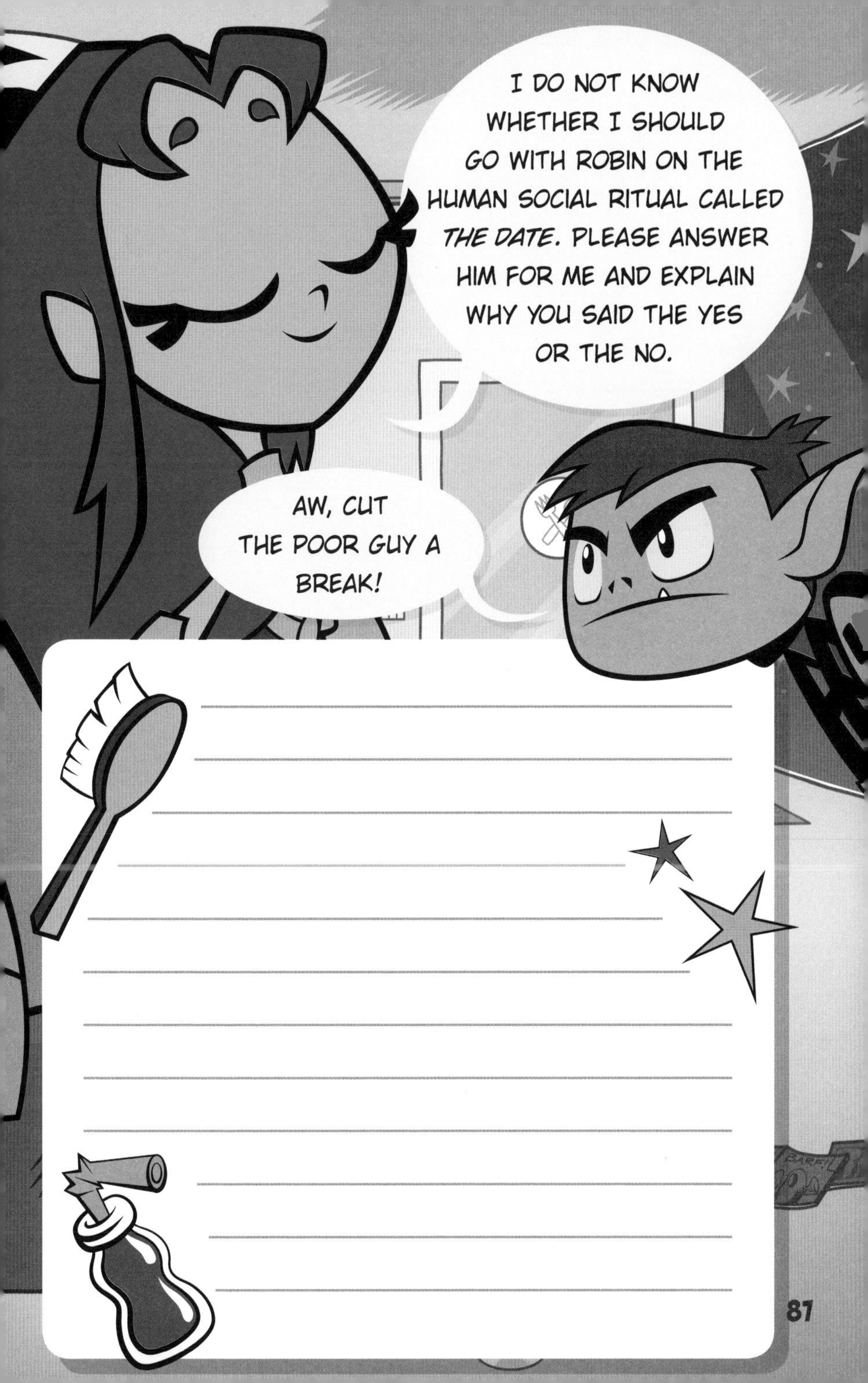
I DO NOT KNOW WHETHER I SHOULD GO WITH ROBIN ON THE HUMAN SOCIAL RITUAL CALLED *THE DATE*. PLEASE ANSWER HIM FOR ME AND EXPLAIN WHY YOU SAID THE YES OR THE NO.
AW, CUT THE POOR GUY A BREAK!

SECRET CODES!

I CAN'T BE THE ONLY ONE AROUND HERE WITH A BRAIN STRONG ENOUGH TO CRACK CODES. USE THE KEY TO SOLVE THESE MEGA-TRICKY SECRET MESSAGES.

A = B
B = C
C = D
D = E
E = F
F = G
G = H
H = I
I = J
J = K

K = L
L = M
M = N
N = O
O = P
P = Q
Q = R
R = S
S = T
T = U
U = V
V = W
W = X
X = Y
Y = Z
Z = A

RNLDNMD NQCDQ RNLD OHYYZ, PTHBJ!

VGN AQNJD LX UHCDN
FZLD BNMSQNKKDQ?

JHKKDQ LNSG HR CDRSQNXHMF
ITLO BHSX!

Now write a secret message of your own.
Share it with your friends!

JHJIKI

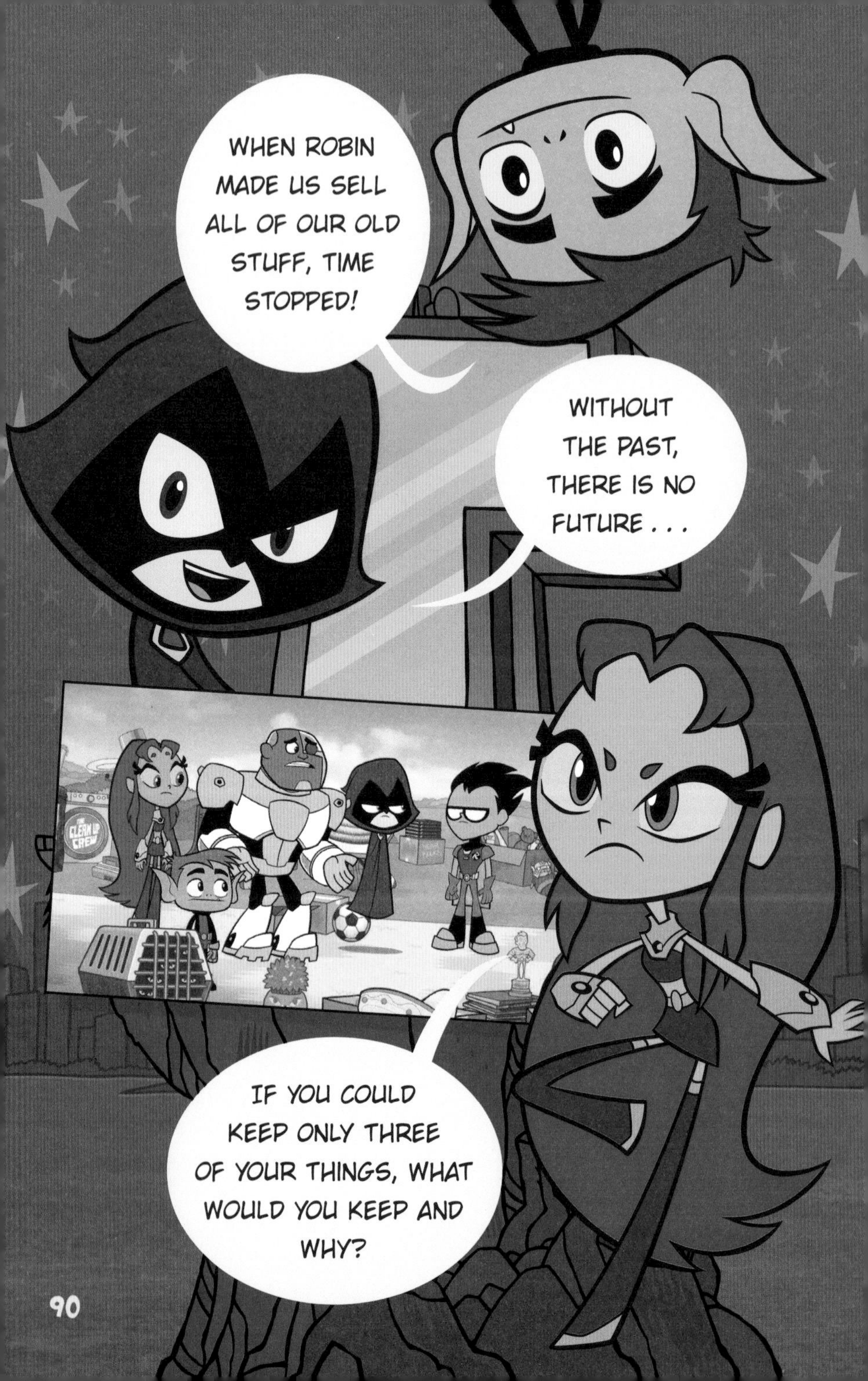
WHEN ROBIN MADE US SELL ALL OF OUR OLD STUFF, TIME STOPPED!
WITHOUT THE PAST, THERE IS NO FUTURE . . .
IF YOU COULD KEEP ONLY THREE OF YOUR THINGS, WHAT WOULD YOU KEEP AND WHY?

THING 1: _____

I'D KEEP IT BECAUSE _____

_____

_____

_____

_____

THING 2: _____

I'D KEEP IT BECAUSE _____

_____

_____

_____

_____

THING 3: _____

I'D KEEP IT BECAUSE _____

_____

_____

_____

_____

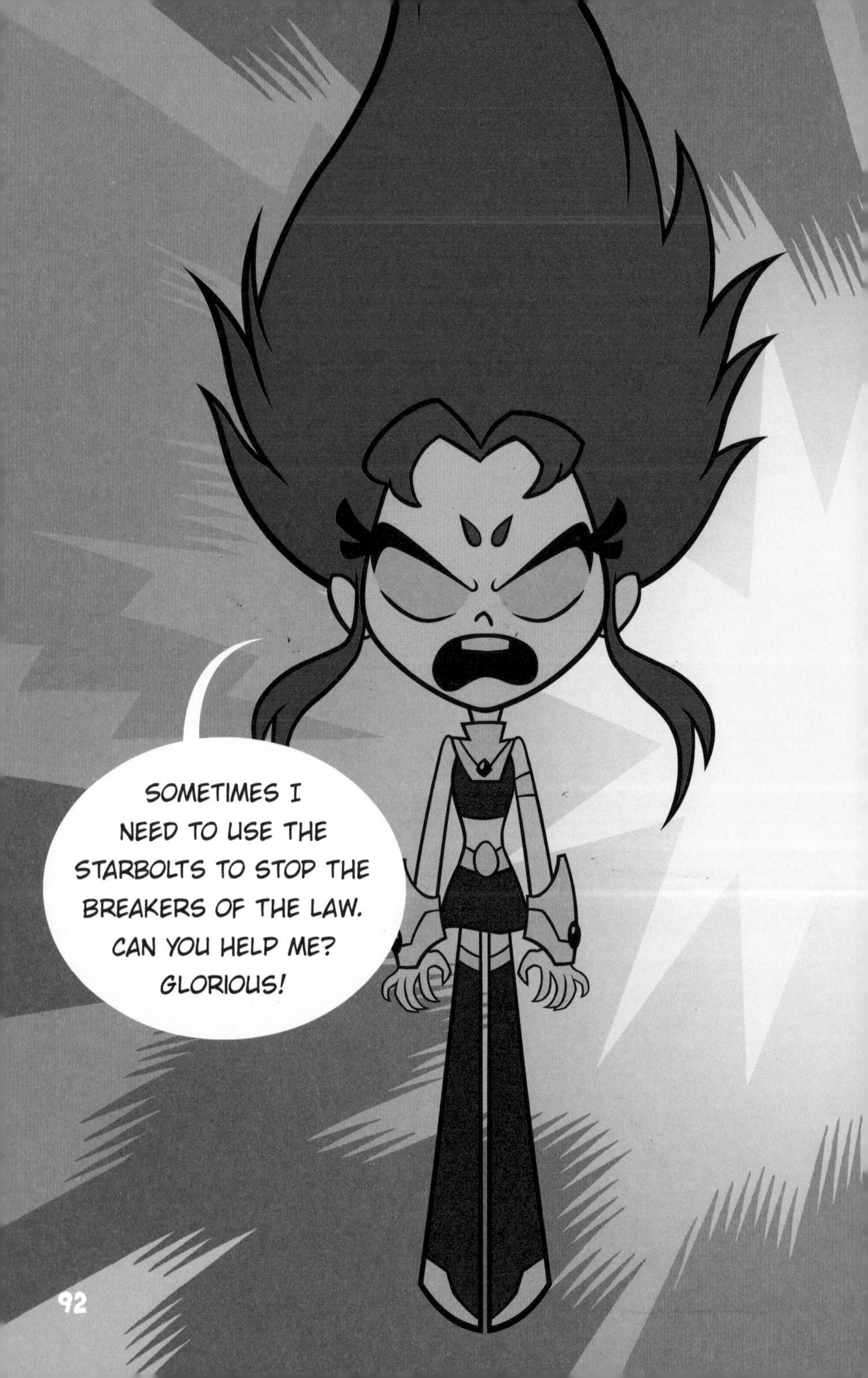
SOMETIMES I NEED TO USE THE STARBOLTS TO STOP THE BREAKERS OF THE LAW. CAN YOU HELP ME? GLORIOUS!

HELP STARFIRE STOP THE BADDIES. PLACE THE TIP OF YOUR PEN ON STARFIRE AND CLOSE YOUR EYES. TRY TO MAKE THE LINE HIT YOUR FOES. HOW MANY CAN YOU HIT IN TEN SHOTS?

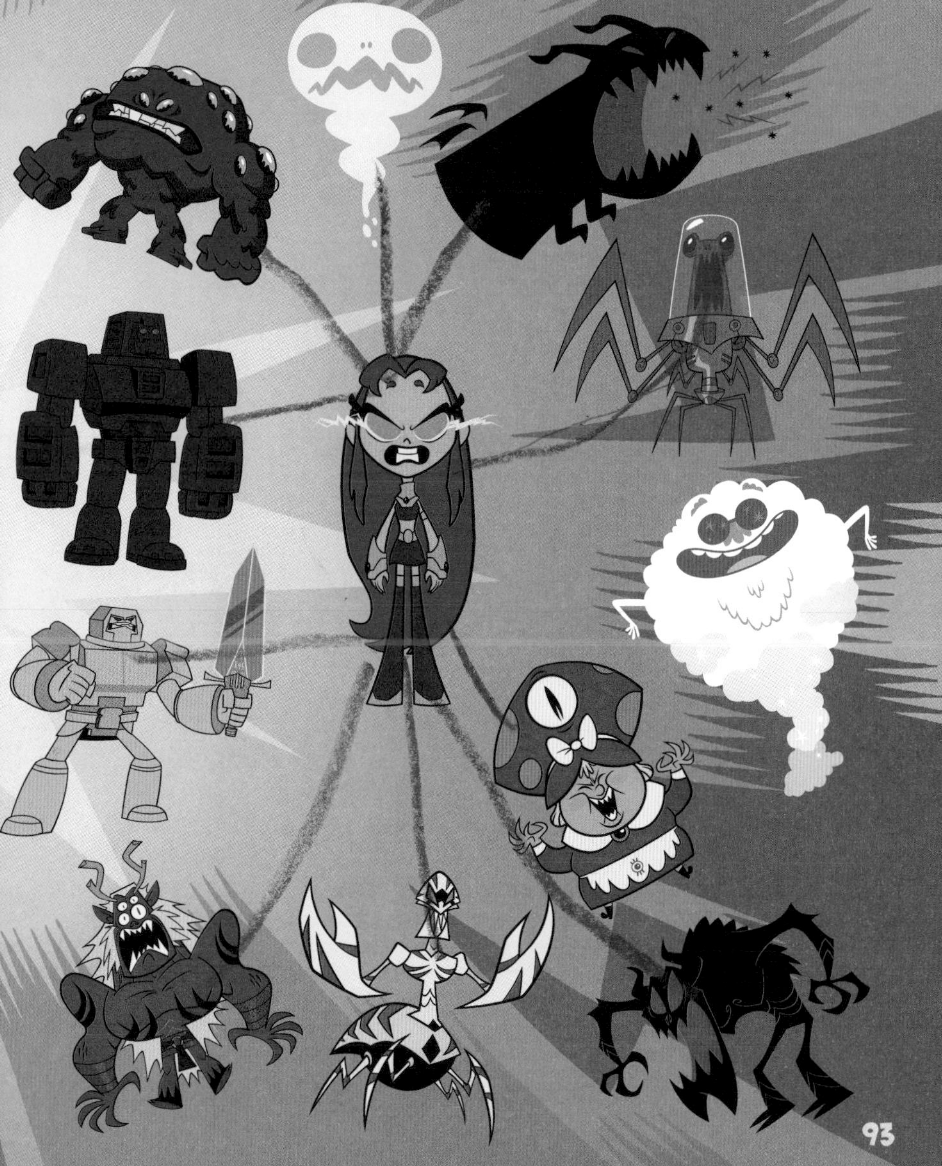

What's your favorite color? Describe a scene using as many things of that color as possible.

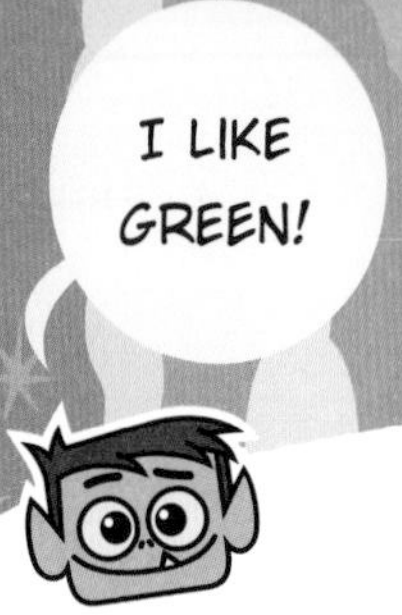
I LIKE GREEN!

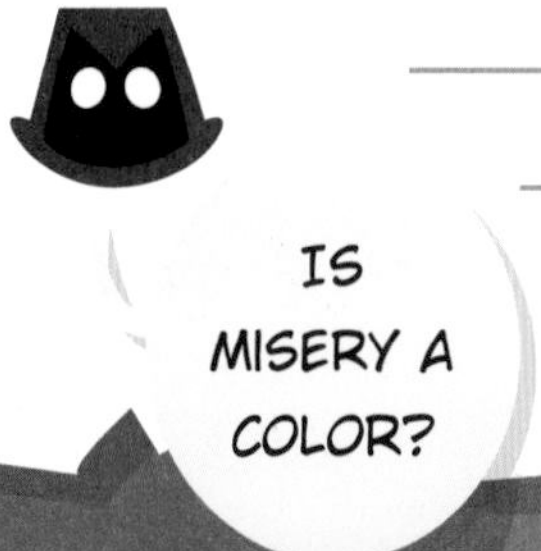
IS MISERY A COLOR?

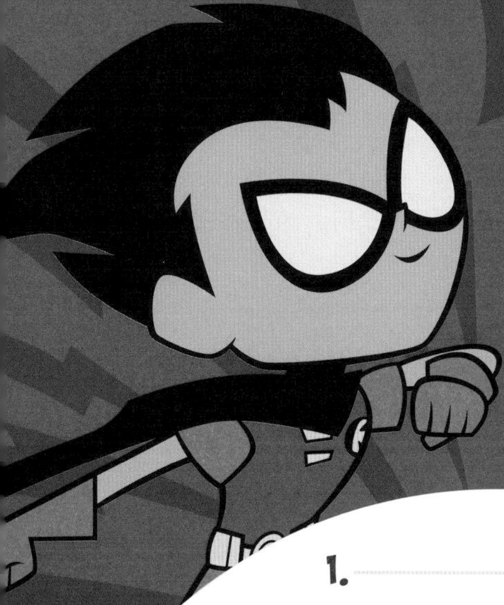

BRAIN NEGLECT IS UNACCEPTABLE. YOU MUST USE YOUR BRAIN OR IT WILL SHRIVEL UP AND ESCAPE OUT YOUR EAR!

WHAT ARE *YOUR* THREE FAVORITE HOBBIES TO KEEP YOUR BRAIN IN SHAPE?

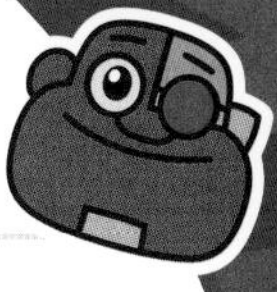
I LIKE MATH!

1. ______________________________

____

____

____

2. ______________________________

____

____

____

3. ______________________________

____

____

____

____

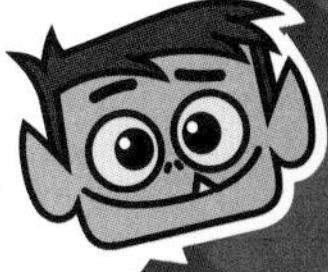
MY BRAIN SHAKES LIKE MARACAS!

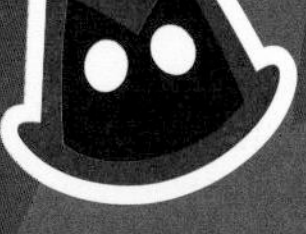
READING, READING, AND MORE READING.

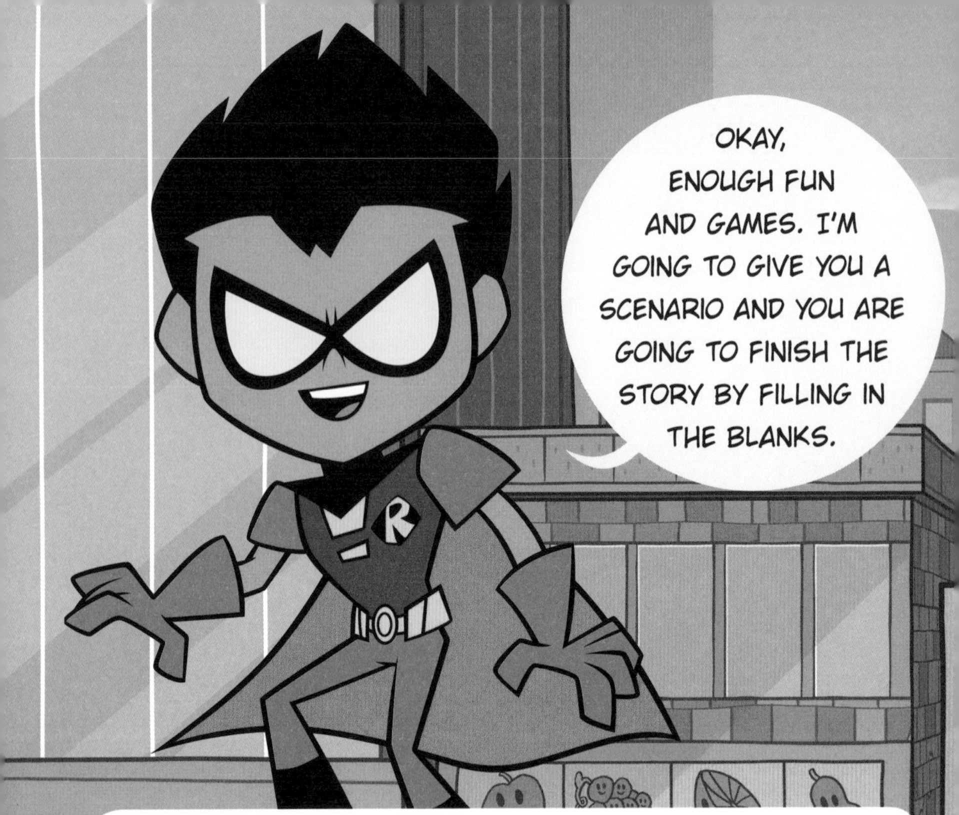
OKAY, ENOUGH FUN AND GAMES. I'M GOING TO GIVE YOU A SCENARIO AND YOU ARE GOING TO FINISH THE STORY BY FILLING IN THE BLANKS.

Once upon a/an ______________ (NOUN), the Titans were hanging out in Titans Tower eating ________ (TYPE OF FOOD) when Robin ran in. "Titans! We have a/an __________ (NOUN)! The H.I.V.E. Five is robbing Jump City National Bank. We've got to _________ (VERB) them!" Cyborg rolled his ______________ (PART OF THE BODY (PLURAL)). "The H.I.V.E. Five is always robbing banks," he said.

"Yeah, chill out, dude," Beast Boy added. "Let us finish our __________ (NOUN)."

"__________ (EXCLAMATION)!" Robin yelled. "We have to leave __________ (ADVERB). Titans go!"

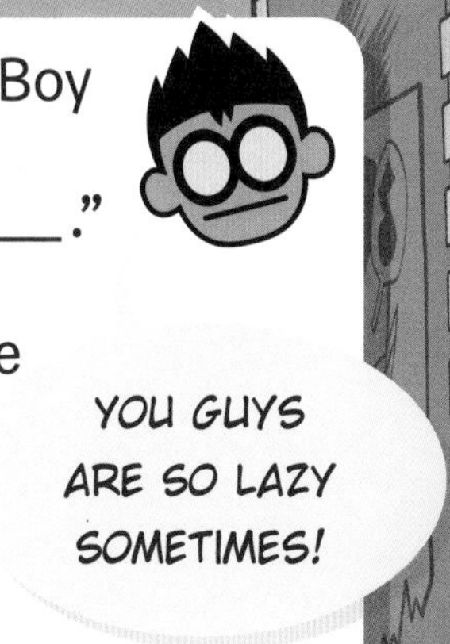
YOU GUYS ARE SO LAZY SOMETIMES!

The Titans sprang into action. Starfire, Raven, and Cyborg flew. Beast Boy turned into a/an __________ (ANIMAL). Robin __________ (VERB (PAST TENSE)). When they arrived, the H.I.V.E. Five was loading a truck with __________ (ADJECTIVE) bags of money. "Stop right there!" Robin exclaimed. "You're going to (the) __________ (PLACE)!" "I knew you'd __________ (VERB)," Gizmo said. "That's why I've prepared my __________ (ADJECTIVE) robot army!" Suddenly a bunch of __________ (PLURAL NOUN) flew down from the sky and attacked.

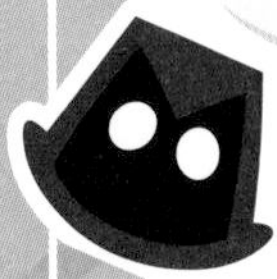
MAGIC
RULES.

Raven yelled, "Azarath Metrion ________ (SILLY WORD)!" and a giant black ________ (NOUN) magically appeared, smashing the robots to ________ (PLURAL NOUN). Then, Cyborg launched a/an ________ (PART OF THE BODY) missile and stopped Gizmo. See-More zeroed his eye on Beast Boy and fired his ________ (ADJECTIVE) laser eye at him. Starfire ________ (VERB (PAST TENSE)) it with a/an ________ (ADJECTIVE) blast of her own. Robin tossed a Birdarang, ________ (ADVERB) cracking See-More's eyepiece. Billy Numerous crossed his arms. "If only I'd brought a pack of jerk-seeing murder dogs," he said. Raven began chanting a spell, but Billy Numerous multiplied

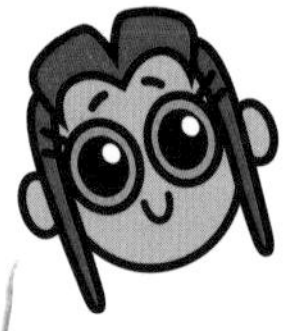
THANK YOU
FOR THE HELP,
ROBIN!

into ___1___. Beast Boy transformed
NUMBER

into a/an ___cat___ and knocked them over like
ANIMAL

___dangerty___ bowling pins. "Woo-hoo! Strike!"
ADJECTIVE

Beast Boy said. Suddenly, Jinx blasted a hex at

Cyborg and a bunch of ___ovals___ popped off him.
PLURAL NOUN

Smoke ___shot___ out of his ___legs___ and
VERB (PAST TENSE)   PART OF THE BODY

he fell down. "My legs are ___orange___!" he said.
ADJECTIVE

That's when Starfire swooped down and kicked

Jinx into the back of a/an ___bike___. "That will
VEHICLE

hold her for the while," Starfire said. Raven cast

a spell that turned the ___bike___ into a cage.
SAME VEHICLE

"That will hold her longer." "Okay, Titans," Robin

said. "Gizmo. See-More. Jinx. ___Inperson___. That's
PERSON IN ROOM

four of the H.I.V.E. Five." Beast Boy scratched

his ___arm___. "So, that leaves only . . ."
PART OF THE BODY

99

The ground shook. The sidewalk ___Ran___.
VERB (PAST TENSE)

A fist knocked Starfire, Raven, and Beast Boy into the bank.

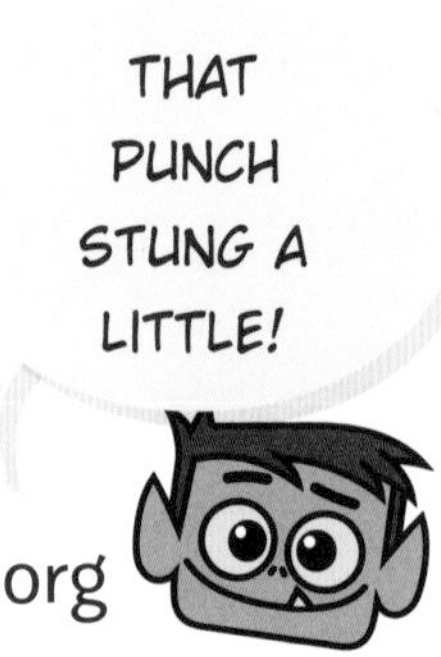
THAT PUNCH STUNG A LITTLE!

"That leaves just me and you," Robin said. "What about me?" Cyborg screamed. "You're lying ___[illegible]___ on
ADVERB

the ground," Robin said. "This is something I have to do alone." Robin threw __________ Birdarangs,
NUMBER

but they bounced off Mammoth's __________
ADJECTIVE

skin. He punched Mammoth in the shoulder, leg, and __________, but Mammoth just
PART OF THE BODY

laughed. Mammoth lifted his __________ fist and
ADJECTIVE

prepared to smash Robin. Robin __________
ADVERB

shut his eyes. That's when Cyborg launched __________ rockets from his __________.
NUMBER PART OF THE BODY

When they exploded, Mammoth went __Runing__ (VERB ENDING IN "ING") through the air and landed in (the) __Tower__ (A PLACE). Robin rubbed his head. "I . . . I guess there's no *I* in the word *team*," he said. The rest of the Titans came out of the bank. Beast Boy turned into a giant __bug__ (ANIMAL). Raven and Starfire put Cyborg on Beast Boy's back for the trip back to __banana__ (SILLY WORD) Tower. "There's also no *I* in the word *booyah*, either!" Cyborg said. "Now let's go have some __pizza__ (TYPE OF FOOD) and __Run__ (VERB) some video games! I need to relax!"

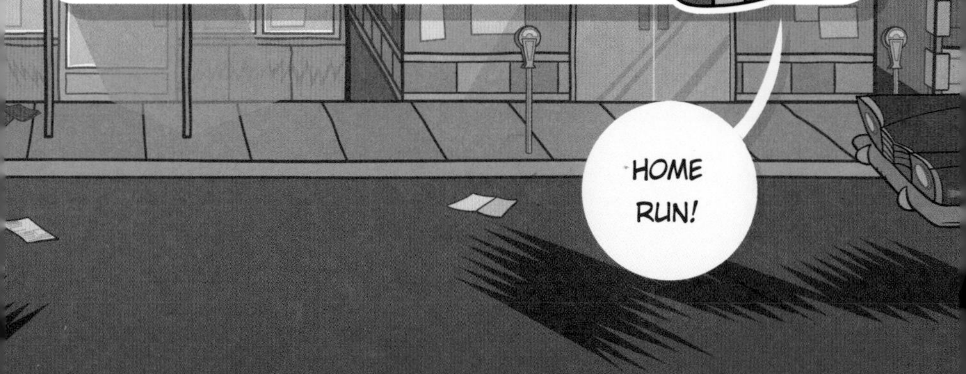
HOME RUN!

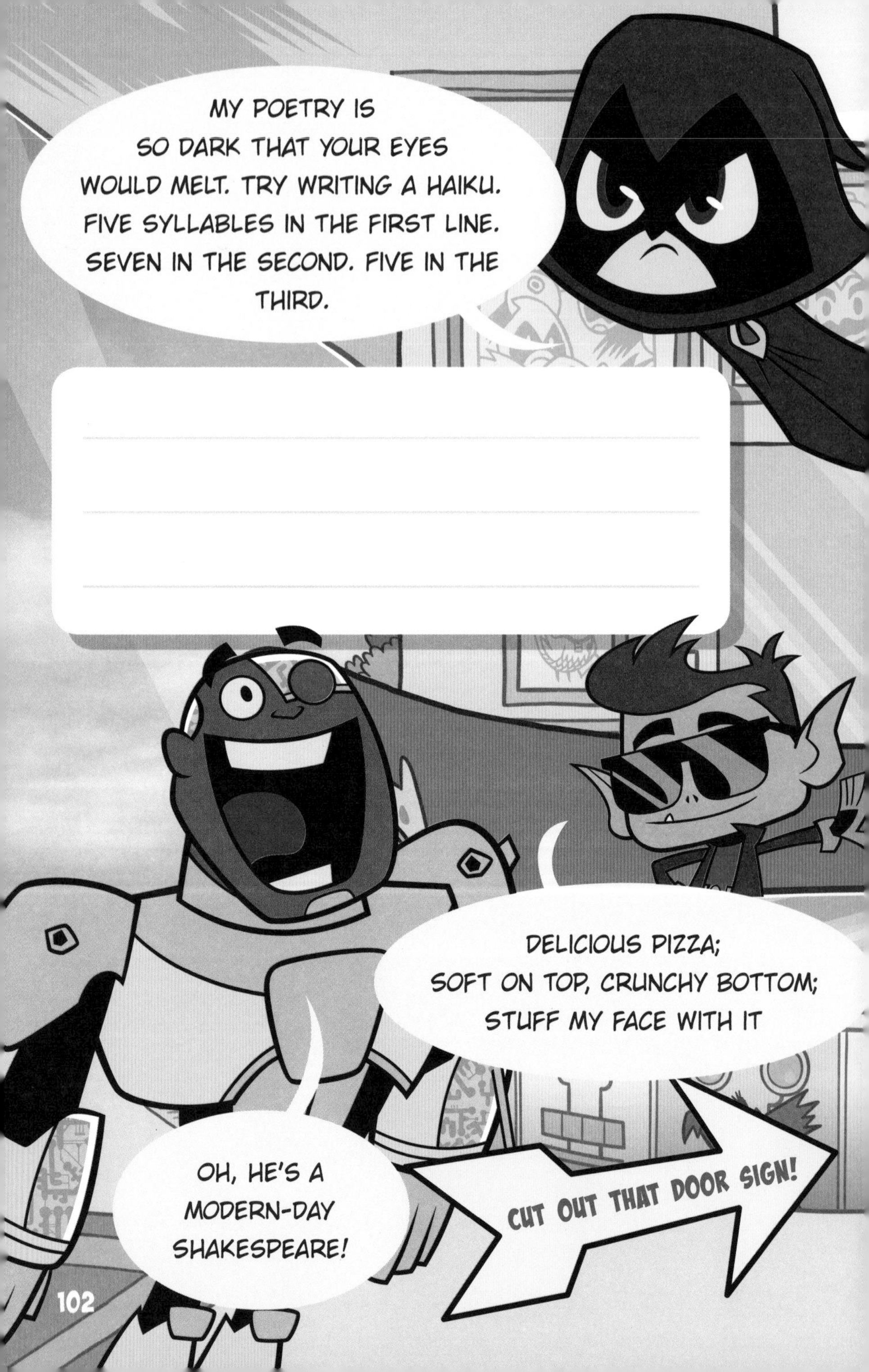
MY POETRY IS SO DARK THAT YOUR EYES WOULD MELT. TRY WRITING A HAIKU. FIVE SYLLABLES IN THE FIRST LINE. SEVEN IN THE SECOND. FIVE IN THE THIRD.
DELICIOUS PIZZA; SOFT ON TOP, CRUNCHY BOTTOM; STUFF MY FACE WITH IT
OH, HE'S A MODERN-DAY SHAKESPEARE!
CUT OUT THAT DOOR SIGN!

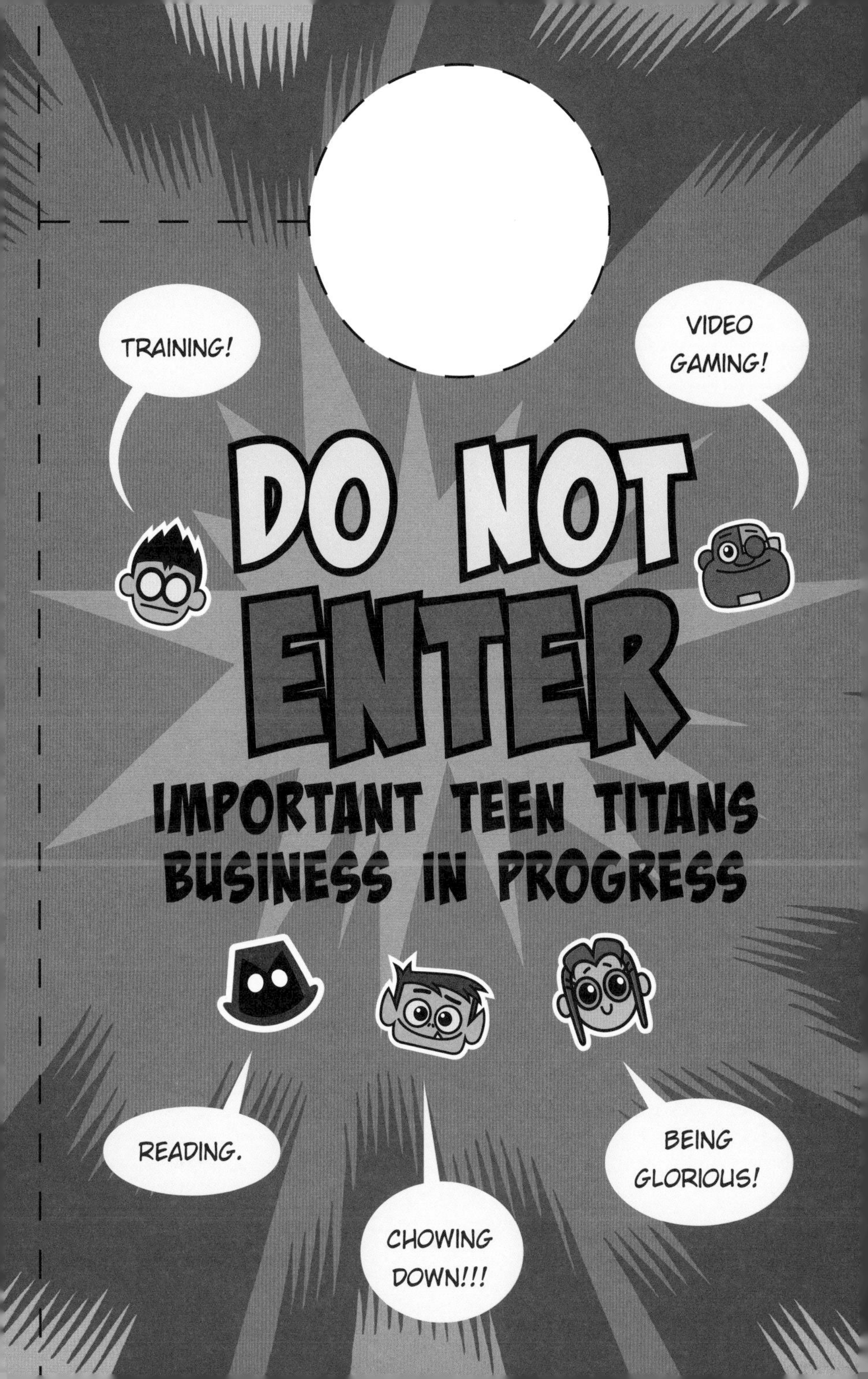
TRAINING!
VIDEO GAMING!
DO NOT ENTER
IMPORTANT TEEN TITANS BUSINESS IN PROGRESS
READING.
CHOWING DOWN!!!
BEING GLORIOUS!

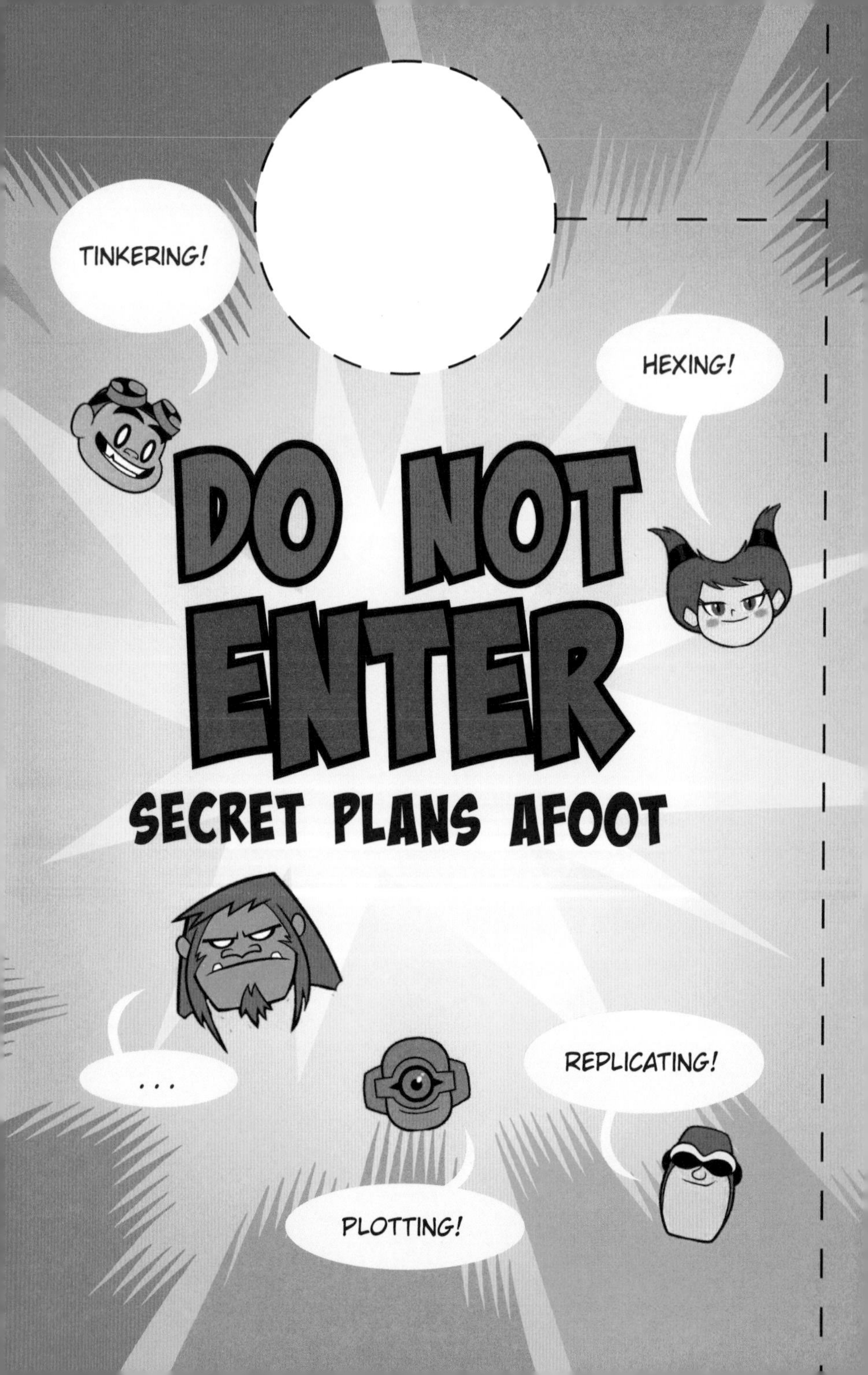
TINKERING!
HEXING!
DO NOT ENTER
SECRET PLANS AFOOT
...
REPLICATING!
PLOTTING!

ROBIN BELIEVES RAIN COMES WHEN THE CLOUDS GET SAD AND CRY. THE TITANS DO RAINY-DAY ACTIVITIES TO CHEER UP THE CLOUDS AND BRING BACK THE SUN. LIST FIVE THINGS YOU LIKE TO DO ON RAINY DAYS.

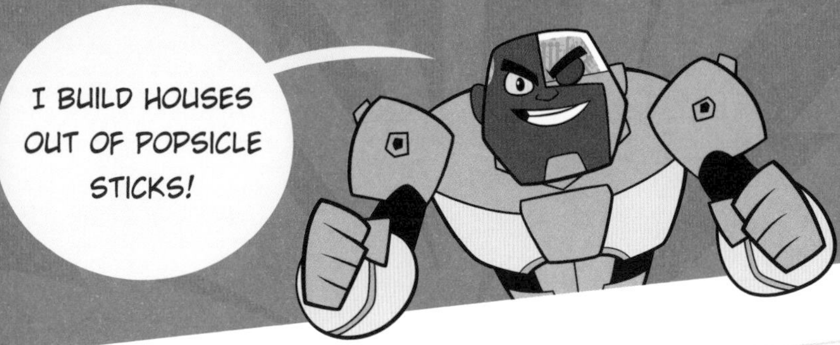
I BUILD HOUSES OUT OF POPSICLE STICKS!

1. ______
2. ______
3. ______
4. ______
5. ______

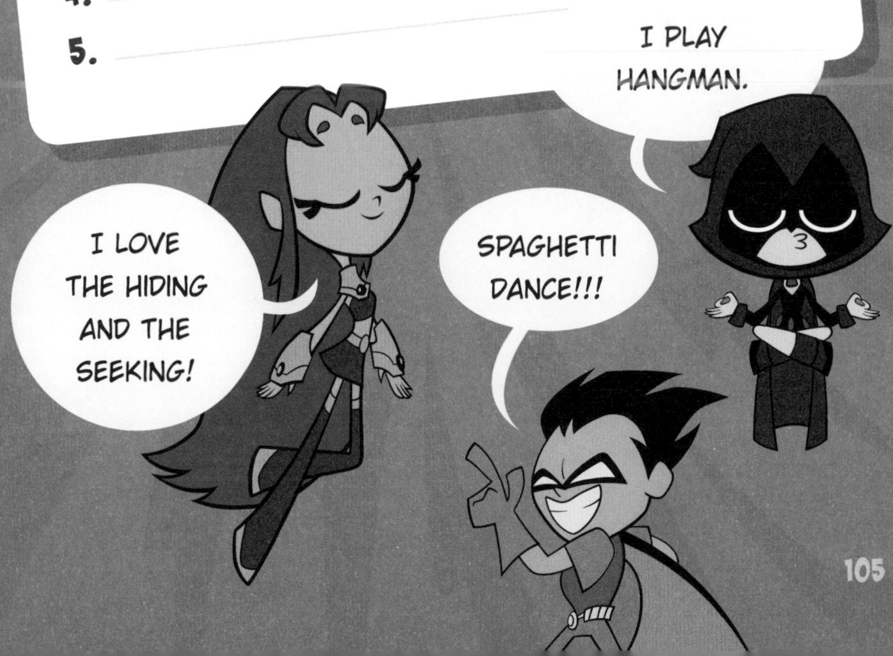
I PLAY HANGMAN.
I LOVE THE HIDING AND THE SEEKING!
SPAGHETTI DANCE!!!

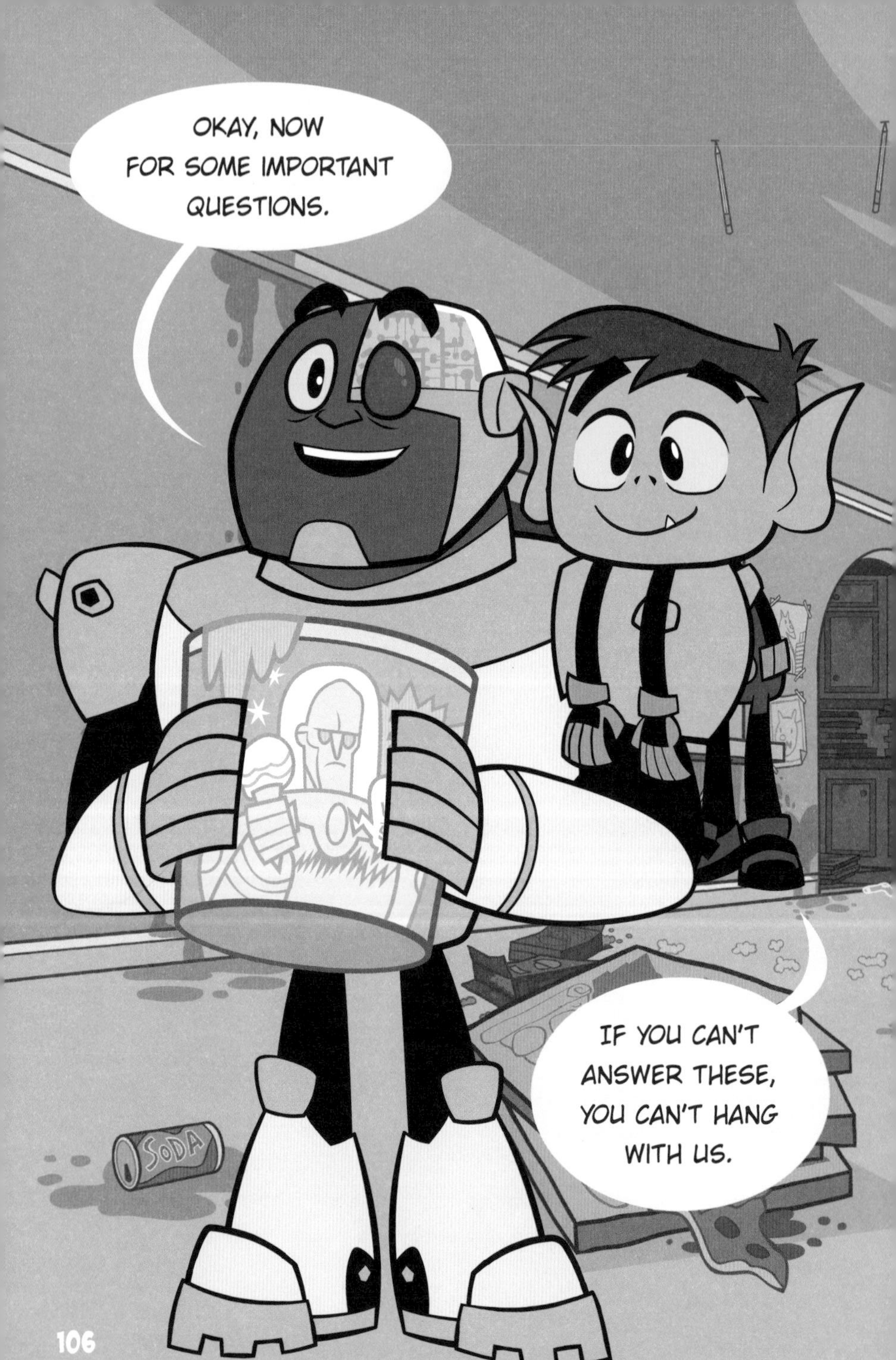
OKAY, NOW FOR SOME IMPORTANT QUESTIONS.
SODA
IF YOU CAN'T ANSWER THESE, YOU CAN'T HANG WITH US.

IF YOU AND TWO FRIENDS CAN EAT FOUR PIZZAS EACH, HOW MANY PIZZAS WILL YOU NEED TO ORDER?

_____

IF EACH PIZZA HAS EIGHT SLICES, HOW MANY SLICES ARE THERE IN TOTAL?

_____

IF EACH SLICE HAS THREE MUSHROOMS ON IT, HOW MANY MUSHROOMS ARE THERE IN TOTAL?

_____

NOW, IF I EAT ALL THE PIZZAS, WHAT NUMBER DO YOU DIAL TO GET MORE FOR YOURSELF?

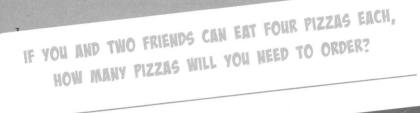

IF YOU ATE ALL THAT PIZZA, CYBORG, WE'D BE CALLING AN AMBULANCE!

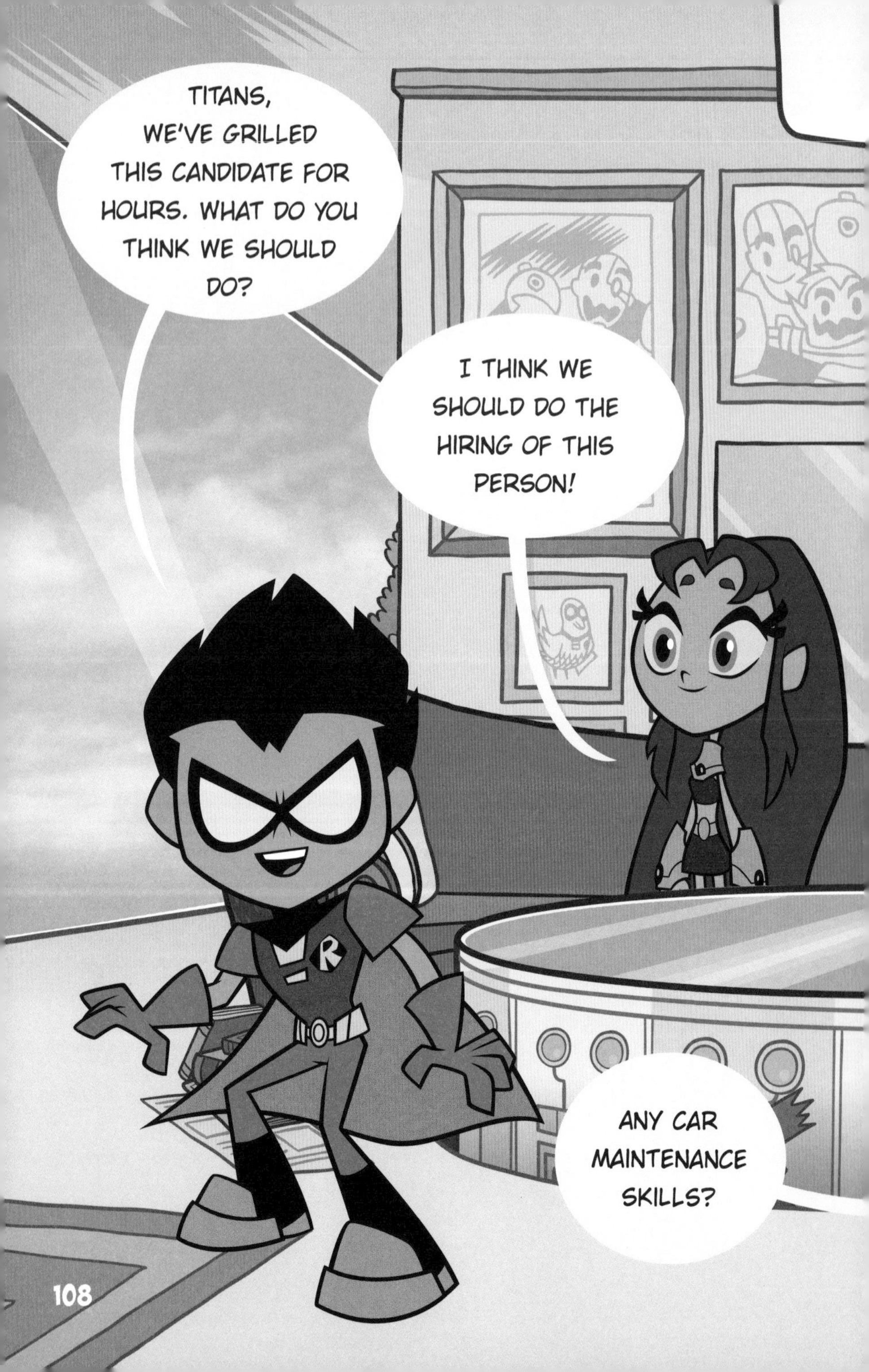
TITANS, WE'VE GRILLED THIS CANDIDATE FOR HOURS. WHAT DO YOU THINK WE SHOULD DO?
I THINK WE SHOULD DO THE HIRING OF THIS PERSON!
ANY CAR MAINTENANCE SKILLS?

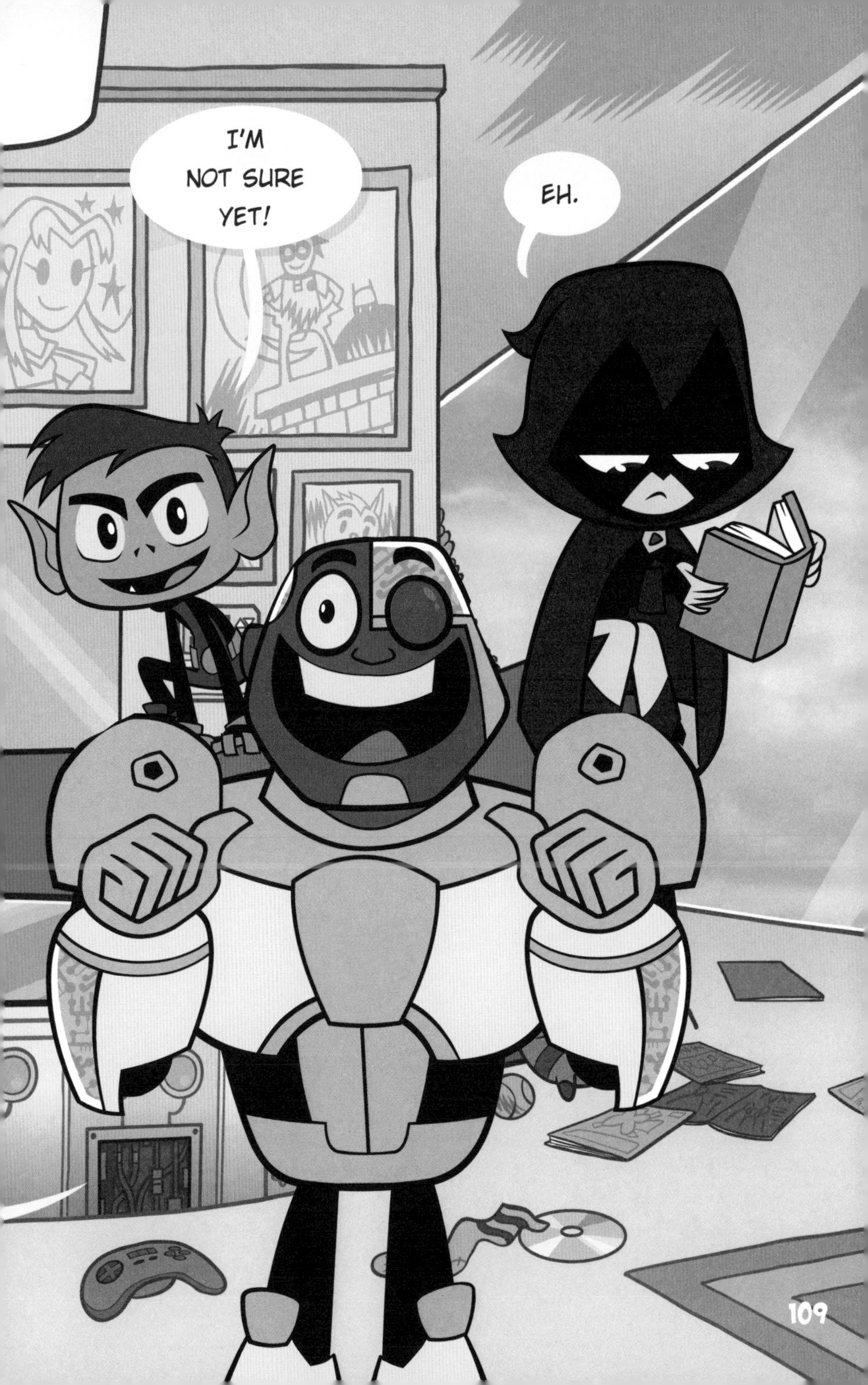
I'M NOT SURE YET!
EH.

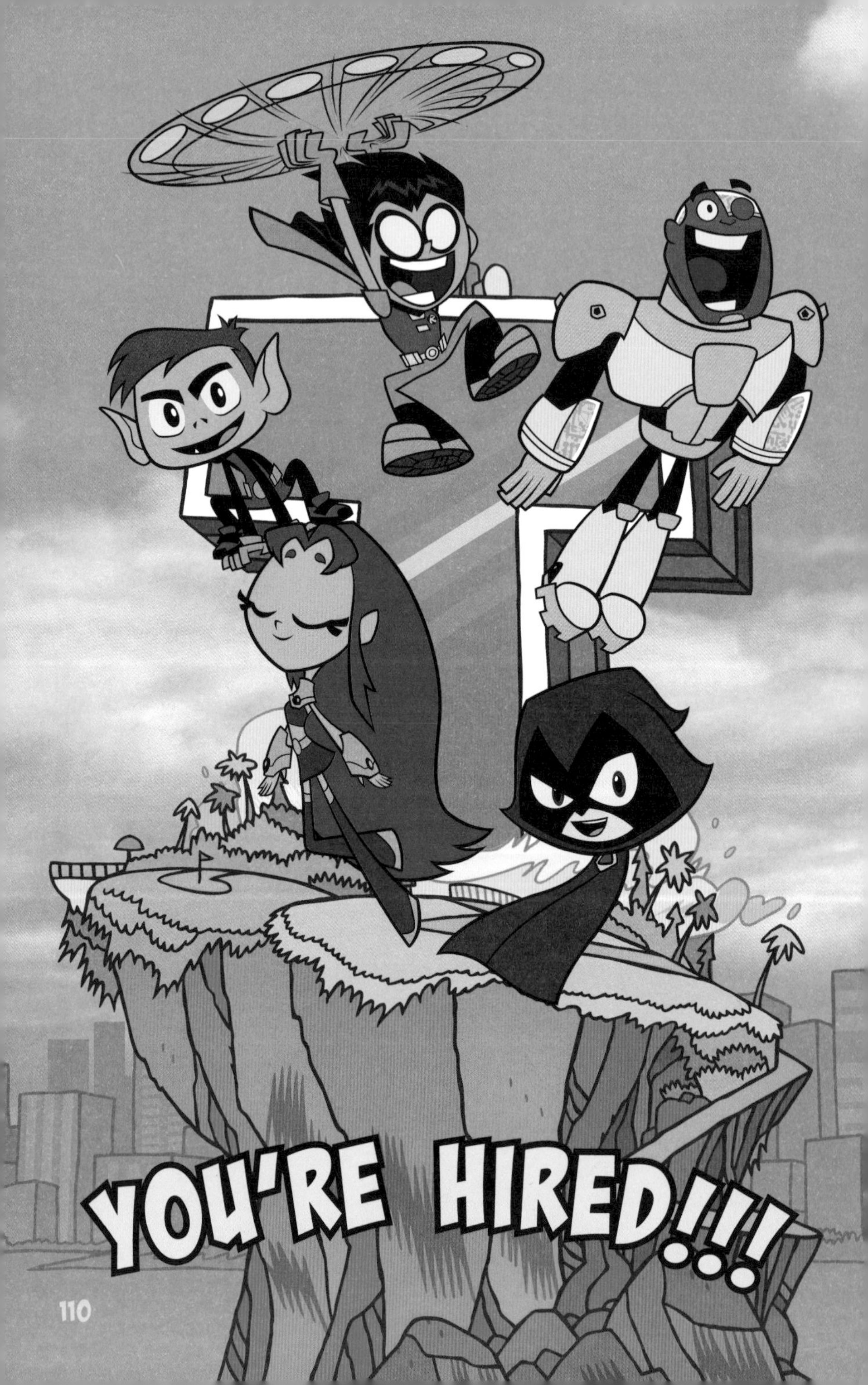
YOU'RE HIRED!!!

ANSWER KEY

Pages 18-19

C	A	Q	U	A	L	A	D	S	T
Y	N	A	Z	T	H	I	V	E	E
B	E	A	S	T	B	O	Y	E	E
O	V	R	U	R	P	M	D	M	N
R	A	R	R	I	T	Z	E	O	T
G	N	E	P	M	A	I	E	R	I
A	N	T	E	N	S	G	P	E	T
M	A	M	M	O	T	H	S	S	A
X	N	I	J	S	R	O	B	I	N
G	O	E	R	I	F	R	A	T	S

Secret Message:
TITANS GO

Pages 8-9

Page 23

Page 36

GIZMO	RIDDLER
SLADE	PLASMUS
BLACKFIRE	SEE-MORE
JOKER	JINX

Pages 48-49

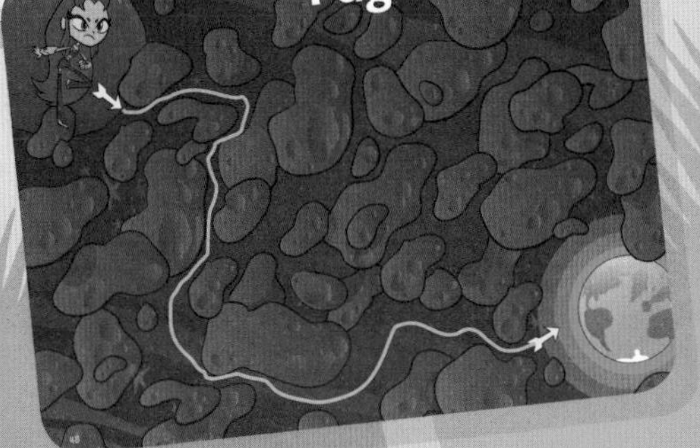

Page 56

Page 84

Page 57

Body Multiplication–
Billy Numerous

Incredible Strength–
Mammoth

Technological Genius–
Gizmo

Awesome Vision and Eye Blasts–
See-More

Cursing Objects and Hex Blast–
Jinx

Pages 88–89

SOMEONE ORDER SOME PIZZA, QUICK!

WHO BROKE MY VIDEO GAME CONTROLLER?

KILLER MOTH IS DESTROYING JUMP CITY!

Page 107

12 pizzas 96 slices 288 mushrooms

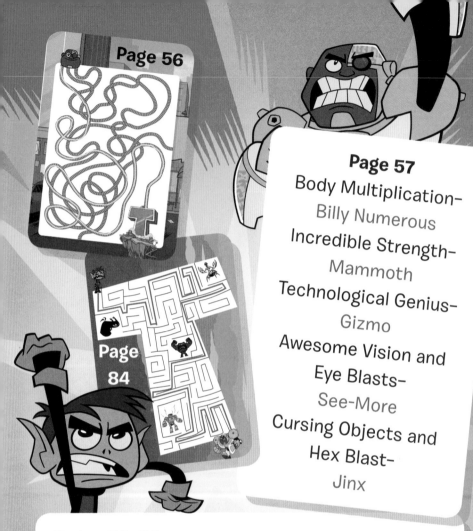